# Playing Friends

**Marilyn Duckworth**

V
VINTAGE

A catalogue record for this book is available from the National Library of New Zealand.

A VINTAGE BOOK
published by
Random House New Zealand
18 Poland Road, Glenfield, Auckland, New Zealand
www.randomhouse.co.nz

Random House International
Random House
20 Vauxhall Bridge Road
London, SW1V 2SA
United Kingdom

Random House Australia (Pty) Ltd
20 Alfred Street, Milsons Point, Sydney,
New South Wales 2061, Australia

Random House South Africa Pty Ltd
Isle of Houghton
Corner Boundary Road and Carse O'Gowrie
Houghton 2198, South Africa

Random House Publishers India Private Ltd
301 World Trade Tower, Hotel Intercontinental Grand Complex,
Barakhamba Lane, New Delhi 110 001, India

First published 2007

Design: Elin Bruhn Termannsen
Cover photograph: Photolibrary
Cover design: Matthew Trbuhovic
Author photograph: Anna Macfarlane
Page 270, quotation from 'High Country Weather' by James K. Baxter, published in
*In Fires of No Return*, OUP, 1958, © J. C. Baxter.
Printed in Australia by Griffin Press

*The author gratefully acknowledges her debt to Peter and Diane Beatson for the Foxton Fellowship, which assisted in the writing of this book.*

*T*here's only one of me, which was puzzling when I tried to pull myself together in 2001, the year New York fell apart. I feel in bits, for some reason, like dropped popcorn or exploded glass. How can the 1950s schoolgirl, only child of aging parents, also be the middle-aged mother of adult children? How can the wife of my first husband possibly have the same DNA as the wife of my second? In bits, you see. Lately I've come to the conclusion I've felt this way all my life. I don't always understand where people are coming from — left or right, underhand or over the top. I can't read faces without my finger tracing and my tongue out. Asperger's Syndrome, I hear you ask? A is a fashionable letter today — Alzheimer's, anorexia, antioxidant, Asperger's — but I don't think so, no. Otherwise how would I have managed up until now, hiding the tricks and angles I've needed to pass in the crowd unchallenged?

What crowd, you ask. And well you might. For a capital city Wellington has a small population. The school we went to had a stunted roll in the fifties. We? Una and me.

'If it wasn't for that screw we wouldn't be here, would we? Not together anyway,' she said to me the other day. True. That much was true. As for the rest . . .

Lies come in a variety of colours. I've told my fair share of white lies, but it wasn't until after the 2001 reunion that I even began to understand how real lying was done, and why.

I'd been striding to join the other women from my class when a lens fell out of my glasses and I had to go down on my knees, riffling the damp lawn. Ah — gotcha. But the wee screw that held the lens in place resisted arrest and I was left with wonky specs sagging under one eye, an eye that I needed to squeeze shut to get any kind of a spyhole on the world. Damn. And so that was how I looked in the form photo. Lopsided, pale-lipped, peering to see if the photographer was ready to take aim and shoot me. Gotcha. Fifty-nine years of Clarice, that's me. Marmalade hair feathering white peppered cheeks — your classic redhead.

We laughed over that photograph later when we were unpacking our boxed-up lives in the flat we'd carelessly decided to share. Una could afford to laugh — she wasn't in the shot because she hadn't been in my class. She was two years younger and a class below me all the way through school, but there she was in her own group photograph, smile immaculate, chin tilted to disguise its plumpness, contact lenses tenderly in place.

'Why didn't you take them off? Silly bitch.'

'But I wear glasses, don't I?' The silly bitch had done it again, told the truth, the easy option. I'd never thought of telling the truth as an affliction before, as laziness pure and simple. But it was.

True enough that most of my childhood was spent behind correcting lenses. I didn't see it as a handicap. It hadn't stopped me getting invitations to the pictures, to school dances, to the downtown Adams Bruce milkbar in Willis Street. Most of these came my way on the school tram where I'd earned a sort of reputation for sharing homework answers with less clued-up kids. Why not? If you smiled at people you got a smile back, or something like. The boys nudged up against me. One of the tram girls said she envied me my squelchy hair or perhaps it was the ribbons I tied it with. Anyway, no one minded my funny glasses. In the evenings I took these off and wrote cryptic entries against the names in my diary. Dick. Stephen. Rupert. While I slept in my schoolgirl's pink bedroom they reconfigured themselves as Mr Darcy, Heathcliff, Robin Hood.

Una hadn't known any of the boys I met in the Adams Bruce milkbar. She was too busy. She spent her lunch hour solemnly swinging a Slazenger, her eye attached to the arc of a flying ball as if it might slip out of her control should she look away. Mad that it mattered so much, but that was Una. By 2001 she had dropped all the balls and didn't seem to give a damn.

In our day the school roll was limited and the faces

above the tartan tie tended to clutter the memory like stamps in an album you could open over and over again. In 2001 at the reunion so many familiar mugshots were flashing at me like junk mail. Even some quite ancient-looking crones wore recognisable features — they might have been in the upper sixth when I was in the third. Could I become a crone in as few as four years' time? Shit. I was only just getting used to being a grown-up. That day I sidled up to Una and peered at the label pinned to her bosom — I always thought of her curves as a bosom — just to be sure. And there she was snatching a sideways squint at my own name tag. We were zoo animals, usefully labelled, but there's a limit to what can be fitted onto two square inches of card. And how many name changes are allowed? I'd had a couple. I remembered Una as the little fat girl who wanted to be a tennis star. I tried to think what memories she might have kept in her head about me. I could see her face collapsed in laughter when I threw up noisily on the house colours in morning assembly. She'd remember that day — and what else?

The day I lost the screw Una had said, 'I've got a paper clip. Here. That's what Jack Duckworth used to hold his glasses together on Coro Street.'

Only months after the reunion we were sharing a flat.

'What screw? Oh, that screw. My bloody glasses. Yeah.'

'You sound like life's all about screws. I wish,' said Una. 'You might be lucky still.'

'How many men you seen me with lately?'

'Okay, no screws. Is this why we're falling apart?'

'We're not falling apart. Well, I'm not.' I had a vision of myself with paper clips attaching my arms, my hands. I flexed my wrists, checking for carpal tunnel syndrome. 'We don't need men to hold us in place.'

Una pulled a face. 'Shit no. Well, actually I'm not sure. I don't like being fifty-seven years old and undesirable. It's a bit like losing your bus fare. Okay, so we've got legs but it's not nearly as good as wheels, eh. Men have carried me most of my life.'

'What are you talking about? You've got a car.'

'I don't mean that. I don't mean money things.'

'So what then? Sex?'

'Fuck sex. I only ever used it to make friends. I thought that was what it was for. It was a nice sort of hobby while it lasted. I miss it.'

'Una! That's truly shocking. It's called making love, remember.'

'How much love have you made? Have you counted? Mum told me it was a lonely cruel world but I proved her wrong, didn't I? She used vodka and Valium but all I needed was a razor cut and a Wonderbra. I had it made.'

I didn't ask where all these friends were now. I saw curvy Una wearing see-through shirts — she called them 'see-mores' — and belted dresses while men queued and fell on her like tin soldiers attacked from behind. Sharing yourself around is a hazardous hobby. I did a bit of it myself before I married. But we're not talking

Aids or chlamydia here, we're not talking unwanted pregnancies or morning-after-pill-initiated fatal blood-clots. We're talking love. The worst kind of hazard. Our friends in the sixties had sex as a rule, but some of them insisted on 'making love'. It was a risky choice of words: making love can create a feeling as surely as a TV ad can create a longing for a cream dessert, as surely as a TV film, based on a true story, can create tears. Sniff. There it goes. The predictable human reaction. Right?

I spared a moment feeling sorry for Una because she minded being undesirable. But was she? She was a bit fat and certainly over-egged in the make-up department but men fuck anything, don't they? She must be missing something else. I knew from school days that her mother was an alcoholic and manic depressive, as we called it then; as for her dad, I remembered her quoting his 'back of my hand' and 'a piece of my mind'. It was the war that made him that way, apparently. There were flying curses and sometimes flying objects. She told me once at playtime, 'Mum's learned to duck.'

I misheard and thought she was talking about some aspect of dressmaking.

'You're so stupid!' she told me. 'You don't live in the real world.'

# Beryl

Beryl was also at the reunion — grey-haired, so nearly invisible of course. Beryl understood the cliché that as you grow older you fade, like a photograph. She was sixty-four. The Beatles thought that was old. No one needed Beryl and no one fed her either. Being fed is what happens to loved pets and Beryl was neither loved nor a pet; what's more, she couldn't afford to buy Jellimeat for even the smallest cat. She did her careful grocery shopping during daylight hours, pulling her wheelie bag — she knew it looked pathetic — to the supermarket that was only a few streets away. She was fading at the edges here in this city-fringe suburb where she had lived, in one house and then another, all her life. The Four Square had become the New World supermarket, the cinemas had gone, and so had Mac's bookshop where she had downed so many cups of tea in the back alcove, snoozing for lazy minutes. The tram rails had been removed years ago. But it was the only place that made sense to her.

The trams had rattled around Thorndon Quay to stop at the looming Government Buildings, largest wooden edifice in the southern hemisphere. Beryl's tram wore the signal destination 'Newtown Park Zoo'. They teased her about it at school, suggesting she shared a cage with the monkeys and chanting: 'She saw a squashed banana on the road. She one it, she two it, she three it, she four it, she six it, she seven it, *she ate it.*' While Beryl waited to grow up and marry and miscarry, one child after another, the tramcars rattled and clanged, one tram after another, painted Indian red with lines of gold, past the Creamoata hoarding in busy Adelaide Road — Cream o' the Oat. Porridge is good for growing children, she knew that as a child, but hated it when it glued to her spoon and stuck in her throat. Tramcars with hard, slatted wooden seats swayed past the sweet factory, the hooded shops, the deep hospital steps and the ambulance bay — *hold your collar, never holler, never go in there* — the motorman's step on the foot-gong, his hand on the swan-necked brake handle, the conductor poised on the back running board. If her tram didn't stop, well, there's always another tram, they told her — it's like boyfriends! — swaggering along the rails, past the cheerful advertising hoarding to her city council stop.

She had caught a boyfriend, while her school friends were still riding the trams, and married him while they were still flirting in the tram shelters. He would give her a baby. She needed a baby more than any of her friends, for a private reason — a reason she hoped was well forgotten — and for a while it seemed to be going to happen. But then, after — oh, how many years? — the babies no longer swelled before turning back. The promise of knitted bonnets and cloth bassinets no longer swayed along parallel rails to where she waited under the hoarding — not Creamoata now but Ipana toothpaste — still holding out her hand to remind the motorman in his black serge coat, 'I'm here! I'm waiting!' He might as well have held a scythe as the control lever. Day and night she had waited to conceive. At night the Newtown trams were trimmed with blue-red-blue lights. Blue-white-blue turned off at the Ascot cinema on its way up over the hill. The short, crooked street where Beryl had taken up residence with Donald was straight ahead, closer to the zoo terminus. Donald hadn't lived long in Wellington and the zoo was new to him. In the monkey cages, at the chimps' tea-party, the young married couple had seen primate babies, a dull copper colour like old pennies.

And then in 1964 — the second day of May, coincidentally Donald's birthday — a last, gay tramcar travelled from Thorndon Quay. The last tram in Wellington and the very last in New Zealand, aflare with flags and bunting, black and gold. The mayor was riding that tramcar, an honorary motorman wearing a sleek suit, cheered on by the Tramways Band. It's a long way to Tipperary! She had hung out of her bedroom window and heard the muffled clamour. It felt like the end of something important, a cross between a victory parade and a funeral procession. Donald went to the pub and came home at teatime smelling of beer. The next day Beryl recorded her last miscarriage in her diary and gave up sleeping in her husband's bed. After all, there was a spare divan in the unoccupied 'baby's room'.

Donald no longer needed his weekend job on the trams anyway. He had finished his apprenticeship and began fulltime work as an electrician. From that day he wore coarse striped shirts and was someone else. And so was she. She missed her good-looking tram conductor in his uniform. What Donald missed she didn't bother to find out. She collected paperback romances from the second-hand bookshop where Donald had found her a job, and hid them in her wardrobe.

She had felt old. She was twenty-five.

W idowed,' Una had told me, that Saturday at the reunion. 'Silly word, eh? Sounds so old-fashioned. But . . .' She shrugged a sort of demure apology. I thought, She sees widowhood as an honourable condition. We were eating scones, home baked by a committee of Old Girls, and she wiped crumbs of the silly word from the corners of her glossy mouth.

'Like wife. Can't get more old-fashioned than husband and wife. Oh — sorry.' I remembered I was talking to someone who had presumably been happily married until very recently. 'So how long ago did he . . .?'

'Last year. Mm. August.' She lowered her head and began to chew on her thumbnail, something I recognised from school days. There was lipstick residue on her fingertip. She had finished the last of her scone.

'It must be hard living with memories. Is that why

you're looking to move?'

'What? Oh no, nothing like that. We hadn't been in that house very long as it happens. I had to sell the place but it wasn't any sort of a wrench, not really, not compared to . . .' Back to the thumbnail. 'I've been staying with some cousins in Karori since then, but it's getting a bit crowded. Time to move on.'

When we signed the papers for the flat I was under the impression — a warm thing, weighing on me like a comfortable old eiderdown — that I knew Una. She was a fossil from my solid childhood. Childhood had been a comfortable place with my mother and my father — married to each other, of course — and pocket money and my own bedroom. I'd chosen a kidney-shaped dresser with a padded stool in front because Elizabeth Taylor had one in *Father of the Bride*. I saw Una as solid and reliable too, barring the familiar tricks of old age. After all, I'd known her — well sort of — for nearly forty years. At school she was one of the sporting types, admirable, mentioned warmly in assembly. Her sort could be relied on to feature in the yearly sports-day calendar and grin from photographs in the school magazine, while I only figured once in a drama production, nearly out of shot. We studied the school magazine before we moved in and there was Una, chin angled smugly. Who better to share an apartment with?

'It goes like this,' she had said. 'You're nice and I'm not so nice. You're no fun exactly but I can live with that. So why don't I? Men die first anyway. We could be good together.'

And then suddenly there was another person in the flat, a clumsy teenager with a loose belly and a big voice, when she wasn't submerged, gluey eyed like a drunk, under the influence of her Walkman. Shit, a cuckoo in my nest. But not for long. Sheree would be giving up the baby for adoption, thank God, and could find her own way in the world from there. She'd be sixteen going on thirty, as Una was fond of saying, and eligible for a youth benefit, if she was unemployed, which seemed likely. She had no qualifications and no ambitions to acquire any, according to Una. She could take herself off to share a flat with others her own age once she'd got herself sorted. So six months at most.

'I should have made it clearer that Sheree would need to move in with us. Are you really okay with it? We can hardly turn the kid out on the street in her condition.'

*'She's making the moves, no hooks, no con. She's getting connected but he's so gone. Here comes tomorrow, going down, going cheap, she wrapped the babydoll for the trash heap.'*

Sheree wagged her head to the Walkman.

I combed the apartment snatching up the detritus of this creature just turned sixteen, Una's 'little cuzzie'. Carelessly pregnant. A discarded rag of panties in the bathroom, a mangled Red Bull can and half a muesli bar under a sofa cushion, chewing gum clinging onto the rim of a kitchen cup.

'She's not really my cousin,' Sheree muttered. 'You don't believe that do you?'

'Pardon?'

'Yeah — well, we're sort of related, eh?'

'What are you saying?'

'I don't like that curry stuff. Do I have to have curry? Call her up on her mobile — she won't mind. The pizza place is right next door.'

I stood very still in the kitchen. I was making up my mind whether to be disturbed by Sheree's disclaimer of cousin status. This wasn't the first time she'd confused me. The last time it had turned out the girl was quoting the words of a rap song, her favourite distraction, and they made no sense at all. She'd roared with laughter when I responded literally.

'Come on, call her up. You must have the number.'

'Sorry.' I made sure I didn't sound sorry. 'She'll be driving back by now. That's the way accidents happen.'

'Oh yeah. You don't like me, do you? I'm not worth a phone call.'

'It's got nothing to do with it. You ate curry happily enough last week.'

'I didn't actually. I spewed up. I am pregnant, you know — I have to be careful what I put in my mouth. Never mind the other holes.' She giggled. 'I bet you don't even know who the father is. Didn't tell you that, did she? Well, it's her bloody Tyler. Fourteen years old and full of it. Pretty good, eh? Bet she didn't tell you that. But who cares who did it?'

Sheree continued to talk in her flat, singsong monotone but I'd stopped listening. I had to deal with the kitchen mess, rinsing the lunch dishes under the hissing cold tap above the waste disposal and slamming the door of the dishwasher so that the faulty catch caught.

'You're not listening, are you?'

'What?' I relented then. 'Look, Sheree, I know you like the idea of shocking me with your stories but you're not going to get very far with that. Despite what you think I haven't always been fifty-nine years old . . .'

'Fifty-nine. Fuck.'

'And besides being sixteen myself once upon a time, I've had kids that age so it's all quite boring really.'

'Been there, done that?' The girl gave an ugly, rumbling snort. 'As if!'

'Una's my friend, Sheree. I don't think much of the way you use her and then sling off at her when her back's turned.'

'Sling off — what's that mean then? Shit, here comes curry. I can smell it. Yuk, yuk!'

She was right. The rimu door swung, pressed open by Una's round forearm slung with aromatic plastic bags. The girl hovered, greedily watching steamy gravy slopping into the deep Chinese serving dish. She reached across to ladle a heaped amount onto a plate, rested it above her belly and headed for her bedroom.

'So where are you going with that?'

'I've got to eat, don't I?'

'Sheree doesn't like curry,' I told Una, raising my eyebrows at the amount the girl had taken.

'She likes everything with calories.'

'Some things I like better than others,' Sheree muttered.

'Yup. That's the way life goes,' Una agreed. She shouted after the girl. 'Don't leave the plate under your bed!'

At the table Una shut her mascaraed eyes while she ate, signalling satisfaction. The room was noticeably expanded by Sheree's departure, silence creeping back into its corners like sunshine replacing shadow. The shiny sofa cushions became softer, rounder, the light in the window gentler.

'So who's this Tyler?' I asked Una.

She sat up straighter. Her eyes were wide open now. 'What's she been saying?'

'Says he's the father.'

'Yeah, well he is, as far as I know.'

'You know him?'

'Yeah. Knew him.'

'So he's not related to you?'

'Is that what she said? Clarice, you don't have to listen to what Sheree comes out with. She makes things up. It's a way of getting attention. Can't help herself. If you listen long enough she'll say the opposite. It all goes round in circles and comes back as something else. Don't let it get you, Claz. It's only for a few months, eh?'

'But you must believe some of what she says? You told me she's giving the baby up for adoption. Are you sure that's going to happen?'

'Yup. Sure I'm sure. I've seen the papers. She'd never manage on her own with a baby. She's a selfish sixteen-year-old looking to have a good time and she won't get that here. Relax. If she turns difficult we'll get her out some other way. I won't let it go on and on. I promise.'

# Beryl

Beryl, who had been alone for nearly twenty-six years, since Donald left her for a yellow-haired bank teller, sometimes woke in the night and panicked because he wasn't in the house, not even in another bedroom. There was every chance she would die alone. Perhaps she would have a stroke and find herself unable to move, unable to cry out. And who, anyway, would she cry to? When she was seven she was immobilised with cramp in the school swimming baths and nearly drowned. She had swallowed her voice. The water turned black over her head and she was threshing in a narrow tunnel while steel chains tightened and clanked about her ribs. Now when she panicked at night she woke tearing the chains from her chest and dragging on the curtain beside her bed. One side of the floral cotton had stretched. She planned one day to take down the left-hand curtain and exchange it for the right-hand folds of blue cloth, but time went on and the curtain lengthened on one side, unchecked.

In the little kitchen, after one of these panic attacks, she confronted the day over the rim of her tea cup, and sent the nasty feeling packing out of the high window. She always used a matching saucer because it mattered.

'I know it's daft,' she said to Greg Preston, a main character from her favourite old television series, who sometimes came and sat at the table with her. 'Help yourself to the sugar. I wouldn't buy it for myself but it can't hurt someone like you. You've never had a weight problem and you're not likely to now.' And she laughed, because she knew it was eccentric to be talking to someone who wasn't exactly there. Or was it Beryl who wasn't exactly there? There were days when she wondered.

She had played with an invisible friend when she was four years old. 'If it was okay then,' she murmured to Greg, 'why not now, when I really need one? I really do need you,' she said and her chin crumpled because she was feeling sorry for herself, which was certainly childish. Her childhood friend had been without gender, like a ventriloquist's doll that had never been fully finished or suitably dressed. It had become something she could fondle and hug, more like a docile dog than a human being.

Greg reminded her that in fact he died in the last TV series, riding off with a nose bleed, bravely planning to infect the enemy with a fatal strain of smallpox.

'I know that,' Beryl agreed. 'Jag har kopporsjuk.' She knew the dialogue by heart, even the bits in Swedish.

'But that was only telly. Telly is lies. Specially reality TV. I know perfectly well you went off screen and had a bath and probably a whisky.'

There was gin, she remembered, in the glass cabinet. But not at breakfast time. Certainly not.

At the supermarket Beryl's trolley passed a woman she felt sure she recognised from somewhere. She wore pleasant, familiar features like a TV personality. Possibly a customer from her days at the bookshop or, more probably, her stint at the local library — this redhead couldn't be more than fifty. Beryl, who had allowed her skin to dry and her hair to fade, regularly misread the ages of other women. In the new millennium sixty might be the new fifty, but not for Beryl. From time to time she encountered past acquaintances and their mild, friendly nods of acknowledgement would degenerate inevitably to a blank response as their lives filled up with layers of more relevant faces. It was hardly worth giving away a smile. She felt safer keeping these for complete strangers like the checkout girls, or for the younger shoppers, the mothers with babies rocking in the carryseats and children diving for lollies at the till.

A second encounter with the same woman at the biscuit shelves elicited the trace of a smile and as it flickered under her nose, Beryl remembered. School. This woman had been at the reunion, flaunting her red hair, more red, in fact, than when she was a small girl in the junior school with a glossy tie and blazer; more self-possessed than she had ever been. Beryl's school blazer had been second-hand, decently faded even before she was enrolled. Now she lowered her thinning grey mop and blushed at the unexciting contents of her trolley. The other woman's trolley was already bulging with French bread sticks, pink chicken breasts and posh ice cream. A shiny eggplant and an outsize pineapple lolled above packets of fancy lettuce.

It didn't matter anyway for the woman had failed to smile back. She was busy waving at her friend, another woman with too much lipstick and a skirt too tight for her bottom.

'Batteries! She said to remind you. For the Walkman. Okay?'

Beryl reached for a six-pack of tonic to go with the gin in the glass cabinet. Mother's ruin. That was a joke. Did that mean gin couldn't hurt someone like her, who had known nothing of mothering? She had talked to Greg at length about her miscarriages, after the break-up when she was first on her own, a separated woman. It was all part of the same loss. The TV series had comforted her at the time, in 1976. The characters — deprived of all that was familiar in their lives by a virus, 'The Death', which had alighted from a Chinese plane at Heathrow — seemed closer to herself than anyone in her daily life. There was really no one else. When Donald went she discovered her friends were actually the wives of his friends — (they listened sometimes to 2ZB and bought *Truth*) — and didn't want to know her. That was the meanest trick of his departure. As well as *Survivors* on the box — the original series, not the silly reality show that had stolen the name — there was the zoo. She could talk to the monkeys. *I saw a squashed banana on the road*.

Ahead of her the till swallowed money with a satisfied 'delunk'. There was muzak on the speakers; voices rose and dipped in Beryl's left ear, which was stronger than her right. On her right the young Indian girl was reminding her to enter her PIN but she didn't hear. She didn't hear because there was a larger noise resounding somewhere in the bowels of the store. Someone was screaming, a high continuous scream on one long note. It came closer. She saw the red-headed woman turn toward the sound and toss her chin up in surprise. Had something happened to the friend with the tight leather skirt? No. A very young girl with cheeky plaits, noticeably pregnant, pranced out of the freezer aisle, her mouth wide open so that amalgam fillings glinted over her fat tongue. The leather skirt was striding behind her.

'What are you doing?' Una asked Sheree, not kindly. 'You're supposed to be at home. Stop it!'

The pregnant girl's mouth dropped shut and spasmed into a satisfied smile. She giggled and shrugged. 'You told me I should get more exercise.'

'I didn't tell you to scream. What have you got there anyway?'

The girl handled two packets of Honey Bumbles. She wagged them cheekily. 'Oh, and this.' A can of Red Bull protruded from her side pocket.

'Sugar. What good is all that sugar for a growing baby?'

'Why should I care?'

'You don't have any money.'

'But you'll buy them for me, won't you?'

Beryl's attention was riveted on this exchange. The checkout girl had given up asking her to 'Enter your PIN, please' and sat back, casting her gaze up at the high ceiling.

'What you staring at, bitch?'

This was directed at Beryl and galvanised her into turning from the scene and noticing the checkout girl's expression. She started. 'Oops, sorry.' She smiled and entered the wrong figure, twice.

She was in the foyer loading the contents of her trolley into the wheelie bag when the three women passed her, calling obscure remarks to each other, as mysterious to Beryl as another language, as if aging were a tunnel into a foreign country. She kept her head down but couldn't help noticing that the pregnant girl had let her top ride up so that an expanse of swollen midriff was displayed to the weather. Her tummy was whiter than her round face. Beryl shivered and tucked her paisley scarf into her collar.

The row of silver garage doors had all been allocated by the time we purchased our apartment so Una was often forced to park the car on a very steep street some distance from our entrance. At this time of day, even on a Saturday, the parking spaces in the street were crammed with vehicles belonging to city workers or customers of the wholesale carpet business along the road. I'd sold my Toyota in view of this and had to rely on Una for transport when we did our weekly shop; it helped to make up for the extra power costs incurred by Sheree. There was a further adjustment in weekly household expenses, which would need to be revised when Sheree went. We didn't talk about Una's finances but I assumed she received some dependant's benefit for the girl. She reached into the car boot, hauling out bags and passing them to Sheree, who at once passed them on to me.

'How's about some money?' the girl asked her. 'Like ten? Or five? I've got a bit, but . . .'

'Where are you going?'

'None of your business. Just coffee money. You can be rid of me, eh?'

Una glared. I juggled fingers into my pocket and pulled out a handful of coins. Six dollars and a few five cent pieces.

'Ta. See ya.'

Una and I balanced a share of the supermarket bags between us and ducked through the swell of airport traffic, running the last few steps with cans and bottles and the pineapple bouncing against our legs. Someone on a higher floor must have left the lift doors open so we gave up waiting and climbed the two steep flights of thinly carpeted stairs.

I complained. 'Bloody hell. We should shop more often.'

'What?'

'If we go more often we won't have so much to lug back.'

'Oh. Right.' Una puffed loudly on the stairs. She had a lot more flesh on her than me and her face sometimes deepened to an alarming shade of red.

'You were right anyway, I have to say.' I hoisted and dumped my share of shopping on the steel kitchen bench, reaching to catch an escaping nectarine.

'About?'

'Sheree. She is nuts. I thought you were exaggerating at first, but no. Definitely bonkers. Certifiable.'

Una, who'd begun to laugh, tightened her mouth in a sort of frown, shaking her fake hair. 'No. Not certifiable.'

'Pity. Someone else could look after her. Someone professional. Or maybe not — in the current economy.'

She screwed up her eyes. 'You can be hard, can't you?'

'What? You can't say you like having her here? You shout at her. I'm just being practical. I'm a very practical person.' I dropped teabags into mugs and switched on the electric jug. 'Remind me — is she your sister's child or . . . And where . . . ?'

'Practical's right. Yeah — a very lucky person, actually. I envy you.'

'Because I'm practical?'

'Goes like this: you're a person who takes things as they come. You take risks. Look at me — this place. I could start ripping you off. You expect things to go right, to work out.'

'They usually do. Well, I manage when they don't. There's always a way of coping.'

'See? That's what I mean. You don't get depressed.'

I felt offended. 'I'm certainly not happy all the time. I get depressed when I have to. My first husband died — I have *told* you. Well, you know what that feels like. We both know what that feels like. But life goes on, doesn't it?'

'You don't know what depressed means.'

I bridled and burnt my lip on hot tea. How the hell did she know what I did or didn't feel? Was she accusing me of having no finer feelings? Then I thought again and looked at Una more closely. 'Do *you*? Know what it means?'

She gave an exaggerated shrug as if her shoulders hurt. 'I did see someone about it once. A therapist woman. Cost me an arm and a leg.' She wagged one arm and one leg. 'See? Very depressing to the bank balance. She gave it a very expensive name. No, I'm okay. If I go down you'll just have to suffer me till I'm up again. I know I can rely on you for that.'

I wasn't sure how to take this. To be relied on is flattering. I might get it wrong sometimes but I'd always made an effort to see what other people were going through. Even Lester had accepted his share of the blame for the marriage rift. And yet I felt a sagging disappointment. I suppose I'd secretly hoped I might rely on Una instead of the other way around. At fifty-nine it would be nice to lean on another person. But cowardly, I guess, and childish.

'I'll do your hair again, shall I?' Una suggested. 'I've come across this new product at work that helps the colour last. Okay? I'm good value in the beauty department. Trust me. Remember Cyclax Milk of Roses?' She'd whizzed through the beautician's course in weeks, soon after leaving school. Was I still the same kind of snob? Probably.

That night I dreamt I'd died and no one had remembered to come to my funeral. In the church pews discarded items — a gaping old handbag, a watch, a crumpled school beret — decorated the wooden seating, but no people. When I woke myself up the wind was blowing, making an eerie noise behind the high window, like some breathy animal escaped from the zoo. The windows were placed high because on this side they looked out at nothing very much, only at other walls with equally high, businesslike windows. It didn't really matter in a bedroom, the place you go to in order to sleep, and dream. About funerals.

I turned over and tried to climb into a warmer dream but couldn't make it. More church pews. Of course I didn't go to church as a rule, only for weddings and funerals. It still pained me to remember David's funeral at the crematorium. The minister had pronounced my name strangely so that I had a sense of being not fully present. It reinforced the aura of unreality that had carried me through the stunned days after he died. I was a figment of the other mourners' imagination, as spectral, as dead, for the time being, as my poor husband who lay there with his hands crossed under the coffin lilies. I moved among them at the wake like Hans Andersen's mermaid, every step a stab of pain, wearing a social smile that only tugged away from me occasionally.

There had been plenty of people at David's 'celebration of life'. But at my own? A few forgotten bits and pieces in an empty church. So I lay there in my comfortable bed — no such thing as a Woolrest in a coffin — making a mental list of friends and acquaintances who were likely to go to my send-off. It didn't look too bad until I eliminated the ones close to my own age and a couple who were conspicuously unfit. Two of my women contemporaries had recently 'passed away', which was surely no more than bad luck, and by the law of averages increased my own chance of longer life, despite my mother's cancer. My children of course — my son, my daughter — would surely fly home from Sydney and Berlin. Perhaps I should have put something in my new will leaving the cost of return airfare over and above the money that would come to them from the sale of this place, which might take a long time. And Una could be a complication. Oh dear. But I hadn't died yet. It was a dream.

'Wake up!' I told myself, shaking my head against the pillow. The wind made its funny noise again, teasing a piece of iron cladding. I'd never lived in an apartment block before. Safe as houses — the expression had to come from somewhere. A house represented solidity, happiness; it was a place where families lived and nurtured each other. Or that had been my experience until a few years ago when my second marriage dissolved. Lester had said it was my fault for making him compete with David.

'You don't marry someone just to ward off loneliness!' he had shouted at me. 'I was lonely. That's why it had to happen.' He'd been excusing his affair, one of many apparently. Poor bugger. Perhaps I *had* let him down, in a way, wanting too much and expecting fidelity as well.

'Oh God!' I sat up in bed and swung my cold feet to the floor. If I went out to make a cup of something hot — ginger tea to scour the dream out of my mouth? —

would I run into Sheree sprawled on the sofa, spooning peanut butter from a jar, as I had the other day? The apartment was open plan and the bedrooms were the only private spaces. I tucked my toes back under the duvet.

I remembered then what had made me dream that stuff. I'd gone to sleep puzzling over my decision to move in here with Una, wondering if I'd done it again, made a commitment to another person simply to ward off loneliness. For Una did seem to believe the move was a kind of commitment. Not surprisingly after all that legal documentation and initialling. But I confess I signed the papers with a different attitude. Una was quite right when she said I was ready to take risks. I'd seen the purchase and the move as almost certainly stopgap, until something like happiness came along — as it must one day — and took me away with it. Why not? I knew I was still reasonably attractive, as was Una, despite what she might say; it was entirely possible we could both ride new mounts into a new sunset. I'd spent most of my life spurred by hope and optimism and only that horrific once had life let me down. David's death had been a felling blow from left field, one I thought I might never recover from. But I had. Things did work out. Life did go on. So why had that image presented itself in the moment before sleep? The thought — This could be my last place. My last resting place. A narrow slot in a shared building with my name on one of the postboxes, like a plaque in the wall of a crematorium.

*U*na was standing in her slippers at the rear window holding the sides of her head as if she were in pain. I went and stood beside her to see what she was looking at. The wall-length window had reinforced panes up to chest level with metal strands criss-crossing inside the murky glass, a reminder of when the apartment block was a factory and warehouse. Above chest level the view in yellowish tinted glass was to the east and someone's leafy garden, frilled with trees and blotchy with magnolia blooms. A statue with a broken buttock raised one hand in a tiny urban courtyard. The sun was shining. I could see nothing in this pleasant scene to give anyone a headache.

'Are you okay?'

'No.' Her neck muscles twitched but she didn't turn her head.

'Does your neck hurt?' I was thinking of the nearby

hospital's emergency department and the complaints of delays, the reports of verbal abuse cast at staff members since that poor woman had died of meningitis, perhaps unnecessarily. 'I don't want to mention meningitis.'

'Yes you do. I'm not sick. Just piss off, please.'

Sheree was elbows-on-the-table, sucking up breakfast cereal off what appeared to be a serving spoon. She had a very wide mouth, slimy with milk. 'Don't sweat it. She does this sometimes. Must be me. Or Jilly.'

'Who?'

A very skinny young person had appeared in the doorway of the small bedroom. She was dressed in a jean jacket and overalls that seemed to have stretched, unless she had been dieting; a half-full backpack sagged from her arm.

'You off then?'

'Yeah. Ta. I took . . .' the girl whispered, indicating a grey blanket folded under one arm. 'Is that okay? Just for a bit.'

Una turned round. 'Oh, just take it! Okay?'

'She didn't disturb anyone. Why are you so snaky?' Sheree wondered, when the visitor had gone. 'Sometimes you really piss me off. She was sleeping rough.'

'Una's entitled,' I pointed out. 'You do exploit her kindness, Sheree.'

'She's not kind. Not specially.'

'No,' said Una, surprisingly. 'I'm not kind. I'm a fuckin' bitch. I don't know why anyone puts up with me, I really don't.' And she strode off to the bathroom where she slammed the door behind her. There was a groaning noise behind the door but it was only the cold tap being turned on hard.

It was Sunday and down the road the carillon bells were ringing out a ponderous sacred melody. The day of rest and DIY. Cars were already parking on the street below, their occupants heading for No Name Building Recyclers along the road. From the Basin Reserve cheerful noises from some sporting event flew up like gulls. That year I was working only four short days a week as a receptionist for a private audiologist. It was a temporary job I'd snatched at wildly when I lost my PR position because the government sold us off; I knew I was lucky to have it. The salary was small but so were the corporate body fees on the apartment and although Lester had walked away with more than his share after our marital split I still had money nervously invested from a modest sum David had left me. I wasn't what was referred to as comfortable — I was quite uncomfortable rather a lot of the time, when the bills came in — but I was okay. About normal. I knew very few people who didn't bitch about money — even my father, and he'd been well enough off when I was a child, or pretended to be. If I lost my job and couldn't find another I'd need to go on the dole for six years until I was sixty-five, which was scary. Sixty-five was scary on its own. Don't think about it.

Maybe money was getting Una down, or was it simply Sheree? I still didn't know exactly why she was saddled with the girl, but I'd given up suggesting she talk about it. It disappointed me that she was so secretive. Sometimes she could say stuff that shocked and surprised me, so her hidden flip side was unexpected. I wasn't used to such guarded behaviour. My recent relationships might have been a bit shallow, certainly in my new job, but at least there'd been plenty of talking and easy opening of cupboards and closets, and I'd hoped for more of the same. I remembered the earlier talk of depression and Una's insistence that she was the expert on this subject and I should keep my nose out. There was something possessive in her attitude, as if she were jealous of sharing her knowledge. It seemed she was behaving in a similar way now, deliberately holding me at a distance. Was this a manifestation of her depression?

I reminded myself of all the years in Una's life when I hadn't seen her and hadn't known who she was trying to be. Who had she become? All I knew was that after her first marriage she went to live in Mangakino, a construction town miles from Wellington. I knew that from back in the sixties. Never mind. I felt fairly sure she would tell me more when the time was right.

I was loading lunch dishes into the dishwasher when her voice erupted behind me. 'You didn't like the way I spoke to that girl, did you? I saw the look on your face.'

'There was no look on my face!'

'There's always a look on your face. You're so judgemental, I can't lift a finger without your nose going up. As if you've done any better in your sweet life. I know you think I'm unreasonable. I can see you working out what I've got wrong every minute of the day. Sheree and her goings-on are my responsibility, not yours. And, by the way, I don't let her exploit me. If anyone exploits me it's you!'

I stood stock still; I think my mouth had fallen open and then a small word slipped out. 'Pardon?' But I certainly didn't want Una to go through it all over again, throw that mess of words, snarled like an old fishing line, into my face a second time. I slammed my mouth shut. 'I have to go.' I dropped the last mug carelessly into the dishwasher and carried myself off to the silence of my room.

My door was shut and I'd had been sitting on the unmade bed, quivering, for minutes. I was trying to hold up the skein of Una's hot words, to untangle them so I could lift out the sense of what precisely had upset her. The 'look' on my face. I went to the mirror and pulled my hair back, searching. My face was empty, eyebrows still hoisted slightly in a floating question. I hadn't put on any make-up yet so freckles stood out on my cheekbones and the nobbly point of my nose.

I stretched out a foot, worrying it into one of the shoes beside the bed. I needed to walk somewhere. 'Shut up,' I said but quite mildly, to the carillon bells, and reached for my shoulder bag.

As I walked I was shedding Una behind me, lingering for a moment at the window of a closed antique shop and coming to a halt at a Lebanese coffee shop where I treated myself to a soothing baklava and 'cappuchina'. I decided I'd keep walking, as far as the zoo where I hadn't been since I was taken there as a kid. The lions' cage had shocked me then with its smell, its confining cruelty, the lioness pacing with what looked like a kind of suppressed anger — or was it hunger? I'd wanted to know and peered to learn the feeding times but Mother had been anxious to get home for a wireless programme. Today the zoo was transformed: there were exotic species, more humanely cared for. I was aware of this from the Telecom meerkat ads on TV. But how many single Wellingtonians would choose to spend an afternoon at the silly old zoo? I congratulated myself on my originality at least.

When I bought my ticket a woman just inside the zoo entrance was talking to an otter which was swimming busily, sleek as a bullet. I nodded at the grey-haired woman because she looked vaguely familiar and walked on towards the nocturnal house which I'd read about in a brochure. I was looking for the kiwi, a bird I would be ashamed to admit I'd never seen. The sun was shining and there were more zoo visitors than I'd expected. In the nocturnal house I was clumsily tall in the company of a stream of children. They chattered in subdued tones probably brought on by the warning notices and the blue lighting. When I emerged into the light a very black spider was spread out on the white wall alongside my shoulder and I jumped violently. Someone laughed and I saw it was that woman again, who'd appeared on the path outside the building as though stalking me.

'Hello,' I said and laughed with her to be polite. 'Big one, isn't he?'

'I can't stand spiders. I think I'll give that place a miss.' The woman moved ahead of me on the path toward the tiger enclosure so that we were walking more or less together.

'You were at school,' I remembered. 'It just came to me. You were a prefect or something.'

'No — never a prefect.'

'Well, someone senior to me.'

'That would be right.' We exchanged names. 'You were in the lower school. And now I'm a senior citizen, discount rate at the pictures. Time does *fugit*.'

'You took Latin? So did I. We're dinosaurs today.' Was I really at school with this old woman? But then I recalled she was one of those at the reunion whose faces I'd filed rudely under the crone heading. Could I be this old in five years' time?

'I don't live too far from here,' Beryl explained herself.

I was searching unsuccessfully for as good a reason for being at the zoo on my own.

'And you?'

'What? No, not really.' I waved a hand vaguely toward the city. 'We're near the Basin. An apartment. I just needed some time out.' Too much information. Beryl didn't need to know what had driven me out of my bedroom that afternoon. If I wasn't careful this woman would be asking me home for afternoon tea. So what was wrong with that? Perhaps after all Una was right — I was a not very nice person with a 'look' on my face.

# Beryl

Sunday was winding down in Wellington. The valleys were wreathed in a greasy late-afternoon shadow, as if some large hand had poured gravy over the inner city. But in Beryl's street the sun was still smiling and smells of cooking, faintly ethnic, wafted across the back fence to where she stood by the rubbish bin, dreaming. The chugging of next door's two-stroke motor mower had petered out now and the neighbour had retreated inside. Beryl was standing with a hand on the small of her back, looking up into the sky where she thought she could see a grey-blue lounge suite settling in the clouds. She could do with a new lounge suite — how nice if it chose at this moment to drop down out of the sky and arrange itself on the rockery at the high point of her garden. She could entertain that woman from the zoo who had been so friendly. Clarice. Beryl shaded her eyes, boring into the cloud formation.

'She didn't want to know you,' Greg said behind her.

'She did. She did. She said we were both dinosaurs. Or did I say it? She agreed with me anyway.'

'The zoo didn't have any dinosaurs,' Greg noted, talking in his tight nasal tones with teeth lightly clenched. There was a laugh at the back of his throat. 'You need to watch out. They might find a cage for the two of you.'

'Oh, pfuh!' She studied Greg who today was wearing his navy duffel coat with that black peaked cap like the Dutch boy who put his finger in the dyke. It was an image that needed to be revised but somehow she couldn't get him to take that coat off whenever he appeared outside like this, even in summer. One of them was getting stuck in their ways. She was moved now to go back inside the house where at least he sometimes removed his hat.

The living room with its speckled carpet had been Donald's place where he would read the *Evening Post*, cover to cover, quite hidden inside its rustling cave of pages, waiting for his tea so that he could get away and hide at the pub, as red-blooded husbands did after the licence laws changed. These days there was no pressure on Beryl to hasten or procrastinate over meal preparations. Greg propped himself on Donald's chair, poised, attentive in a way Don never had been, while she stepped down into her tight little kitchen and reached towards the scantily stocked pantry. Greg wasn't above calling out to her with observations that might interest her. In the alcove her stove, her aging fridge, the coloured benchtops, were close at hand. She had only to swivel in her Hush Puppies to put herself in touch with all that she needed. And she needed so little. It was some time since she had used the paint-spattered stepladder to stretch up to the higher shelves; she had nearly forgotten what was up there. Look out, she said, more to herself than to Greg. That's how it begins, old age, forgetting what's in your own cupboards. But Greg was taller than Beryl: she could leave it to Greg to remember the high shelves.

When I strolled in the city supermarket, browsing the deli section, I was planning a belated housewarming party to cheer Una up — a daft idea perhaps but I'd had a dull day at work and needed cheer of my own. I was reminded of similar impulses to brighten the mood of my Sophie or Stuart, following a poor school report or a failure to make the rugby team. Lester, when he'd inherited these two as teenage stepchildren, was more inclined at such moments to criticise than cheer them, but I was their mother and vulnerable, protective as mothers had to be. Was I still stuck in some sort of mother role? To Una? Certainly not. Her mood affected my own when we lived so close and shared the open-plan kitchen, the same front door; it was no more than that.

I scanned and filed in my head the relative prices on an artist's palette of dips — olive green, orange, warm cream — and transferred a large discount camembert to my basket. Well, you don't need a party for cheese. Perhaps it would produce at least a camera-width smile in Una. While I walked home past the snarl of trolley buses and cars in Adelaide Road I was making a list of people I planned to invite and came up against a familiar dilemma — broken marriages. Secret liaisons I was supposed to know nothing of. People told me things because, I suppose, I was known to be discreet. But there was almost too much in the way of secrets to remember and handle discreetly when you got to my age. And which spouse to invite when both were your good friends? Who was speaking to whom? Who was now Lester's friend rather than mine? Presumably Una would have friends too, which could be interesting. She hadn't mentioned anyone particular yet.

'And we can ask the other people in the building,' I reminded her.

'Can we? We haven't met any of them. They could be awful. They might not want to know us.'

'Of course they will. We're nice.'

'You may be. I turn people off,' Una said. 'I say the wrong things.'

'You're right — you do talk some bullshit. You're at least as nice as I am.' I caught myself glancing towards the closed door of Sheree's room. 'I don't imagine it'll be quite her thing, will it?'

'You mean there's going to be no food? Nothing to drink? She'll be here, no worries. I'll tell her to behave.'

So the party was on.

47

It seemed Una might have been half right about turning people off. Apart from neighbours in the building very few of the people she invited had put in an appearance; in fact I can remember only one — a mauve-pated man who, I learned, had taken early retirement from the menswear department and now stood alongside Una's yellow packet sponge-cake with a dreadful smile on his face. *Are You Being Served?*, I thought. He was wearing new sky-blue trainers and leaned into them first on one hip, then the other; a tired old horse, refusing to sit down. If he was waiting to be entertained he might be waiting some time. One of my friends from my old workplace — where I'd once earned a measure of respect — was making loud, careful conversation with the second receptionist from the audiology rooms, as if he believed deafness might be catching. Una was being burbled at greedily by a middle-aged woman from an upstairs floor. As I approached she brightened rather obviously and made a clumsy attempt at an introduction, preparing to escape.

'Marge,' the woman corrected her. 'But I'm made of the best butter actually.' And moved all over again by her wit she shook inside red silk, a beautiful raspberry jelly. 'I don't see Kevin about. You did invite darling Kevin? The downstairs gentleman? He's a special friend of mine.'

'Yes,' I said, holding firmly onto Una's elbow so she couldn't get away. 'Didn't we, Una?' We were both well aware that the only unattached personable male in the building had been invited. He had been invited twice, a note under his door as well as in his letterbox.

Our front door was propped open with a footstool and now a black streak rippled across the carpet and into my room where the wide bed was heaped with an opulent mound of coats. I thought of the otter at the zoo.

'Only my little dog,' Marge gurgled. 'India! Out of there! I named her after one of my bedrooms, but it does suit her perfectly, don't you think? It's a fancy of mine, doing out rooms to match places I've visited. I've done India and Bali and now I can't decide on France or Spain. Then I've run out of rooms, so I'll just have to stay home, won't I? The living room's England, of course, so it's a little bit dull. God save the Queen. And the kitchen I call Greece.' She giggled. 'Naturally. I never could spell. Oh I'm sorry about the dog, dear. Shall I take him back upstairs?'

Una's lips were already stained purple with the cheap wine — quaffable, she called it — and she was beginning to lurch and laugh at unfunny remarks, some of them her own. When a tall man in his thirties with a stuffy banker's tie briefly interrupted an exchange we were having about supper preparations, she smiled widely and announced, 'I do like your son, Clarice. He's a real charmer!'

My head went back like whiplash. 'He's not my son. I told you — Stuart's in Sydney. Jack's a friend of his. I don't have any family in New Zealand at the moment. I told you.'

'Isn't that often the way? We get left behind, abandoned.'

The conversation chugged ahead, onto grandchildren, then globalisation. I was still stunned that Una could make such a mistake. I thought of the occasions when I'd discussed my family circumstances with her at length — unnecessary length perhaps — and yet so little of it seemed to have sunk in. I could as usefully have poured it down the wastemaster and leant on the switch. It was insulting and hurtful. Unless Una was suffering from premature aging — but she was only fifty-seven, younger than me.

'I'm drunk,' she said. 'Forgive me but I need to lie down. I'll do it in Sheree's room. Feel free to use mine.' This was just as well since her room had been set up to serve as the bar. It was the biggest bedroom and had ribbed glass doors opening off it into the living room. When we moved in I'd been content to choose the smaller double room which was further away from Sheree's little back bedroom and from kitchen noises.

'I reckon they ought to whip the whole thing out and be done. That's what Mrs Fulham's in for, isn't it? It's no use to you now, is it?'

'I'd rather have hung onto . . .'

'No, no! Being a woman — honestly! My cousin had hers out last year. Touch and go that was. She lost three pints over what you're meant to. Couldn't get blood into her fast enough — she nearly went. Her husband almost had a heart attack over it. That would have been the whole family. The daughter'd died just before — she had a heart as well. Awful.'

The party was at a rolling boil now and I was left in

sole charge of the supper, frighteningly more ambitious than I would have chosen without Una's insistence. I checked to see if any bottles needed opening or replacing.

Multicoloured scarves and heirloom jewellery wafted in and out of Una's room, visiting the bar; sunworn faces on tired shoulders, boggy eyes hiding behind mini spectacles that resembled cobblers' glasses. The wrinklies, as the teenager called them, were busy looking after themselves and there was nothing much for me to do except enjoy myself. I had nearly forgotten how.

Sheree had commandeered the best burgundy arm-chair as usual and hung upside down with her pale ankles hooked over the high back, Walkman trailing wires on the floor. *'Here comes tomorrow, going down, going cheap . She wrapped the babydoll for the trash heap.'* Stuart's friend, Jack, couldn't take his eyes off her belly button, which strained at the lime green T-shirt she had chosen to wear. She had worked out in advance that no one close to her age would be at the party and had accepted money to go catch a movie at Mid City but for the time being she seemed reluctant to turn herself right side up and leave. Her face upside-down was comical but somehow more acceptable, her short plaits wagged as she moved to a hidden rhythm. She wasn't listening to the chatter I was stuck with.

'They're dismantling me. My breast, my womb. It's my teeth next month!' Hysterical giggles. 'I told my doctor — you pay more and you get less.'

'I lost my nest egg in the crash. All gone.'

'Humpty Dumpty, eh? Fell off the wall!'

'Can't write a script without looking it up in some book. My old doctor didn't have to do that.'

'It'll be the water next. Watch this space!'

Stirring tabbouleh with my back to the guests I noticed how the bleakness of the dialogue didn't match the cheerfulness of delivery. The subject was now war and death — what else? — but the voices were raised, bright with glee. I was at something like a stage play where the director didn't understand the mood of the writer. Of course gloom is rude at a party.

If there was an earthquake now and all these people were to be swallowed up how much would it matter to me? I knew some of them too well and others not well enough but I couldn't see anyone I wanted to know better. I had felt sure that funny Beryl would want to come, but even she had dithered when we encountered her outside the supermarket car park, laden with our party supplies, excusing herself on the grounds that she'd have to ask Greg. Greg — her husband presumably — sounded the old-fashioned sort, a control freak. He didn't like parties apparently.

# Beryl

On the night of the party she wasn't prepared to attend, Beryl woke in fright, smelling Donald's beery breath on her pillow. She sat up in the dark, reaching for the light switch with a sweaty palm and gulping breaths of good air, for the smell was gone now. Her rapid heartbeat slowed. Not a ghost — her husband wasn't dead — but only one of her dreams, and she wasn't even sure how it could frighten her. She had slept with that breath often enough in the past and it wasn't as if he was ever abusive to his wife, even when she'd taken herself off to her own bed. She'd had to buy a new mattress for the double bed after he had left her for Michelle, because there was a lumpy hollow on one side that was a rude reminder of his absence as well as an ordinary discomfort. His absence, surprisingly, was the most frightening thing of all. She had gone back to his bed nostalgically, as soon as it was empty of him. The feminist literature she had progressed to after she burned her Mills & Boons supplied no answers for this behaviour. Her lack of understanding was as despicable as her reading of formula romances earlier, but there was nothing else to do except read. There wasn't much she wanted to watch on TV these days — it was all about real life and real life had so little to do with Beryl. She glanced hopefully at the paperback lying open under the lamplight, but it wouldn't do. She switched off the light instead and turned over.

Greg, of course, would smell of whisky, never beer, but he had lain down on her bed, only once or twice, when she was especially lonely or afraid. Like the time she had to go to the hospital for a scan, but it had turned out to be a false alarm, as he had predicted. He was kind then. And he hadn't lain too close ever, not close enough to touch or smell, just near enough to keep the bad stuff at bay, so that she could go on breathing.

Tonight she knew he wasn't close at hand or she wouldn't have smelled Donald. She slipped into her chenille dressing gown and went to sit with a cup of milky tea in the back sunporch where she could look at the night garden. In the moonlight the house on the rise and to the left transformed itself into a stone country mansion somewhere in England. Her mother had obsessed about her childhood home in the English Midlands but her words had flared unnaturally with fairytale repetition while this country scene conjured itself into view as easily as opening a window. If she sniffed hard she could smell odours of chaff and dung and she knew that in that dark corner near the compost there was a three-legged stool where Greg sometimes sat milking one of the farm cows.

Beryl had been born and bred in Wellington, like her father before her. It wasn't very patriotic of her to be friends with a man so very English, but Greg had just happened to her at the right time, talking to her from the TV screen in 1976. You couldn't summon up friends at will any more than you could deliberately fall in love. Looking back she saw how she had kept herself proudly aloof, a self-contained unit without silly small talk, when she worked at the library. It was how she was, how her mother had been, not her fault. It hadn't occurred to her when she was younger that pride could leave her alone in an empty house. Quite alone. She shivered as reality reached out clammy fingers and touched her. There was always the radio, but even that had its limits. And Greg?

She couldn't be blamed for needing Greg, just as she couldn't be blamed for taking the odd paracetamol. 'I know you're mad at me,' she said. 'And I know why.'

'So tell me,' Greg answered, moving out of the shadows.

A swelling wave of relief built up in her and broke so that she couldn't help a couple of sobs and had to wipe her dressing gown sleeve under her nose. She sniffed. 'I shouldn't have used your name to get out of the party. But what else was I to do?'

'Go. You could have gone.'

'I couldn't. I would have panicked before I got to the front door. All on my own. I never go to parties on my own. And what would I wear?'

'The dress you bought for the reunion. You were okay to go to the reunion.'

'That was different. No one had partners with them at the reunion, everyone was alone. It was like school.'

'So you're never going to wear that dress again? What did it cost you — remind me?'

The moon slid behind a cloud and for a moment she could hardly see Greg's face. 'Anyway I've done it now,' she said. 'The party is probably over.'

'You've done it all right. How are you going to ask Clarice back to visit when she'll expect to meet your partner in the flesh? You can't, can you? Unless you want to be seen as a liar. Or a nutter. You've blown it.'

As if to echo his words Beryl reached in her dressing gown pocket for a tissue and blew her nose. When she looked up she found she had extinguished him like a candle.

*S*unday again, and the kitchen window was streaming with rain that squittered sideways when there was a gust of wind.

'I'm suffering from post-traumatic party syndrome,' Una said, leaning on the open dishwasher as if it were a walking frame.

'Not a hangover?'

'Okay — that too. What about you?'

'There's a lot of cleaning up to do. Was it worth it?'

'I'm not crawling round the floor after corks and glasses and stuff. My head would fall off. If you want to do it today I'll vacuum tomorrow. Sheree!' Una bellowed at the closed door, then held her head with both hands. 'I told Sheree she could help you. I'll give her some money. What am I saying? I've already given her the money.'

'She's gone out. She borrowed your jacket.'

'Oh. Damn. Well, she'll be back. Has that jug boiled?

We need a cuppa.' Una was wearing a loose nightie that was escaping off one soft shoulder. Without her clever make-up and her tight skirt she looked far nicer, I thought.

'Plenty of people came, anyway.'

'Anyway,' Una repeated. 'Right. It was a flop.'

'What do you mean? The supper was great, by the way. And if you go by the noise level . . .'

'I'm glad you had a nice time. As for that Marge! And Kevin didn't come, like I said he wouldn't. Probably terrified of our beauty.' She snorted sarcastically.

'He's nudging sixty himself.'

'Possibly. So he'll need a forty-year-old at least.'

'I didn't think you had any real plans for him.'

'Why not? I'm desperate.'

'Are you? I think I've had enough of men.' I meant it. 'It's such a chore unless they're absolutely fascinating. Their minds, I mean. But even their minds go mushy. I tried to talk to that man with the bald head — your friend . . .'

'Not really a friend. And he's losing it. That's why he's retired early. Boring old sod.'

I wanted to ask why she'd invited boring old sods to her party, but I thought I knew the answer.

'You're right,' she said. 'I'm not worth knowing. I'm a worthless piece of shit. Don't talk to me. You'll only tell lies.'

I opened my mouth, then closed it again. I launched myself from the comfortable chair and returned to scraping plates and stacking the dishwasher. Una was sitting with her hands around a steaming mug, holding on as if she needed to warm herself. Her chin crumpled and tears leaked into the cracks around her nostrils.

I said, 'You told me not to talk to you.'

'That's right. Get on with your work. I'm not going to help you. I'm a shit, I told you I was a shit.'

As I planted dirty glasses in the rack I was thinking, I listen to you. I remember the stuff you say to me. But you don't remember things I say to you. Important things like where my son is living. Yes, you're a shit. Sometimes.

The dishwasher hissed as it began to fill with water. I moved away, straightening my back to confront the living-room chaos that I'd had been purposely keeping outside my line of vision. Una had already wheeled the big tea trolley laden with bottles and discarded glasses out of her bedroom and cast a mess of scrumpled tea-towels and paper napkins after it. There was a trail of peanuts that looked deliberate, leading towards Sheree's bedroom door. I skidded on a plastic cork and saved myself by clutching at Una's ornamental skinny giraffe. I discovered the top part was detachable and had come away in my hand.

'Look out!' Una blurted, unfairly.

'It's okay — see?' I reattached the head and gave it a mollifying pat. The red eyes stared at us, unblinking. It wasn't something I would have chosen for myself but this was one of the adjustments you had to agree to when you shared your living space. It occurred to me then that I was doing something like flatting, an exercise I'd had to observe in Sophie and Stuart before they'd taken the next step and married, one after the other. It wasn't so different in fact from marriage. I'd secretly nurtured a peculiar dislike for some of Lester's treasured possessions, in particular a Chinese carved fish with bulging eyes. It had been a gift from his old maths teacher and hardly his fault.

Una had retreated to her bedroom and closed the glass doors by the time Sheree got back, shaking the rain from her outdoor clothes like a dog. I stepped clear of this and frowned at her.

'Why don't you hang those in the bathroom?'

'Uh?'

'Una says you're going to help me get this place in order. She gave you some money for it.' When Sheree merely raised her eyebrows and put her head on one side I went on, 'I could really do with some help. And don't think being pregnant is some sort of excuse to laze about and get out of shape, because that's the worst thing for you and your baby. All that loud music won't teach you anything about life.'

Sheree's head was still cocked to one side. 'Anything else?'

For an answer I thrust a cloth into her hand.

'What am I supposed to do with this?'

'Use your imagination. The kitchen bench might be an idea, and after that the stove top. Use plenty of Jif.'

Sheree laid the cloth down. 'Okay, but I'm allowed to go to the loo first. You don't want me pissing on your nice clean floor.' When she said 'clean' she erupted into a sarcastic bubble of mirth and stirred a scattering of potato chips with a toe of her Reeboks. I resisted picking up the cloth again, even though a greasy smear on the fridge leered at me seductively. Sometimes I was an obsessive wiper. The bathroom door remained closed for an unlikely space of time. When I leaned my ear against the saucy French 'Lavabo' sign I'd hung there myself before the party, I could hear running water. It went on running. 'Sheree? Are you all right?'

'I'm running a bath.'

'What? Wouldn't that be better after you've done your cleaning?'

The door wrenched open. 'That's what I was going to do. It just takes so bloody long to fill I thought I'd start now. Okay? Just get off my case!'

'Sorry.' I heard myself apologise, the abject tone, and cringed. I had handled my own teenagers better than this, surely — but they hadn't been pregnant, pretending to be grown up. Sheree was a very confusing person to be around. Sometimes she made me feel seriously out of date rather than adult. My head was aching. 'Give it up,' I told myself out loud, and did what Una had done — retreated to my room and shut the door. Apart from a livid green silk scarf someone had left behind on the bedside table, this room was unsullied. My head on the feather pillow. Bliss.

Someone was knocking on the door. Thumping. I roused myself, thinking of the police. I was a character in *The Bill*, but couldn't remember the nature of my crime. What had I done? By the time I collected myself Una had struggled out of bed to answer the door and stood clutching at the wayward straps of her nightie, darting a startled sideways glance past me towards the alcove in front of the bathroom door. A line of water was seeping from under the crack, darkening the carpet, and when I tugged questioningly at the handle the tide increased. Someone had overflowed the bath.

'Oh my God! Sheree!' Una howled, splashing past me and diving for the taps.

Kevin, the 'downstairs gentleman', was standing on the doormat, flinging his wrists about. He seemed to have run out of words.

I managed to say, 'I'm sorry. Well, come in. Hello.' Everything in the wrong order.

Sheree had snatched the earplugs from her ears and advanced to witness the bathroom drama with her mouth sagging. 'That was your fault,' she accused me, squeezing her fat lips together. 'You interrupted me.'

'Is it very bad?' I asked Kevin. 'In your place?'

'Bad enough. I just happened to look up and there was this big damp patch, spreading . . .'

I listened, trying not to visualise this man sitting on the loo with a soggy *Penthouse* magazine propped open above concertinaed trouser legs. When Una called I gave myself a shake and headed for the linen cupboard and the towel supply to join her in mopping up the floor. To Kevin I called over my shoulder. 'I'm really sorry. You'll have to excuse us.'

'Offer him a drink!' Una hissed from the bathroom. Her nightie was clinging to her, defining the dimples in her thighs, and the bath was flowing with sodden towels, while she handled the sponge mop using powerful muscles I hadn't previously noticed.

For a moment I was silent with admiration. Then I said, 'This doesn't seem like the right time.' And after a quick look around the corner — 'He's gone, anyway. Here, let me have a go. That'll take forever. Sheree can fetch the washing basket for those towels.'

'She can have a go at wringing them first — it's the least she can do.'

'I don't know why you're getting at me,' Sheree said later when we were sitting slumped at the kitchen table, breathing hard. 'I'm sorry, but you wanted to meet the guy and now you have.'

'What do you mean?' snapped Una. 'You call that meeting? He doesn't even know our names.'

'It was on the invitation,' I reminded her.

'Not the same thing. He might think I'm Clarice and you're me.' She considered for a moment. 'Actually, we will have to go and apologise and have a look at his ceiling. Eh?'

'Eh plus,' said Sheree and giggled, surprising me. Perhaps she wasn't as stupid as she made out.

# Beryl

Something was wrong with Beryl's eyes. She must go back to the optician. It was certainly harder to decipher words on a page and the idea that they might escape her altogether was scary. But the optician would remedy that. More worrying was the way her vision was playing tricks on her with Greg: she felt sure she'd seen him more clearly a few years ago. And idiotic as it might sound — she knew it was idiotic — she had the distinct impression this morning that she had witnessed his duffel coat and peaked cap striding away from her, up the road towards the park and the zoo. How could it have been Greg? And yet what real person would have worn such clothes on a sunny day with not a breath of wind?

It was two days since he told her she had blown it. It had rained for all of Sunday but now the sky was as smooth a blue as the inside of Don's favourite serving bowl. She hesitated with her hand on the crooked front gate, watching a young mother approach with her baby slung on her front; she was holding hands with a young fellow in jeans. Not a pram in sight. Surely it couldn't be good for the girl's back? Times had changed. Beryl was propelled out of the gate against her will, timing her step so that she would get a quick look at the child, lapping at the sight as if it were a longed-for ice-cream cone. Cool, as young people say. There — she had known the child must be beautiful with parents like those two. Envy played across her ribs like a piece of familiar music. She shook her head quickly before another nastier memory could crash noisily into her ears.

And when the couple had gone — walking faster than Beryl liked to walk, almost dancing — she continued at her more leisurely pace to the yellow-columned zoo entrance. They must have thought she was mad to buy a ticket so often out of her super — she was aware her blouse and skirt were the garb of a superannuitant. In fact she was still six months away from her superannuation entitlement and until then she was battling poverty. She didn't know how to manage debt as young people seemed to. The zoo should be free for pensioners. Hardly much skin off the nose of the city council and the animals wouldn't mind, might even enjoy it. But today she had another motive aside from monkeys and the solitary bear. Idiotic she might be but she would indulge herself: Greg wouldn't be easy to miss in his curious get-up. Worth looking, anyway. Just in case. He knew it was one of her places.

She had forgotten her purse but the woman let her

in anyhow. She blushed with shame — they would think her a silly old duck and perhaps she was. Too bad. She was in now and the sun was still shining, getting in her eyes. It was Tuesday so it wasn't surprising that there were few people about. She strolled, pretending this was her own garden. If it weren't for the giraffes nuzzling each other and admiring their wonky-legged offspring she could have pretended she was on Greg's farm. And while she was thinking this she remembered a *Survivors* episode that had featured an elephant, escaped from a place like this. Sadly there was no elephant here now — the smelly elephant house she visited as a child had been converted to a sort of educational space with chairs and tables and a drink machine that had no smell at all. She checked out this building, then moved on to the bear pit. One of her childhood books had featured a precocious little bear — Mary Plain — and this sad middle-aged bear looked to her rather like Mrs Mary Plain, disillusioned.

As Beryl reached the rail she had to step backwards to avoid a man in khaki and green who was dismounting from a golf cart burdened with plastic buckets. He wasn't a young man and he looked as if he could do with a new electric razor to get rid of those bristles. She stared at him because while his back was turned and when she blinked he had looked nearly like Greg Preston. Her hand on the rail was slick with perspiration; she put up a damp finger to rub her eyes. She watched while he inserted a large pink pill inside a piece of orange and cast it into the enclosure. Then, summoned by a younger man who waited for him on the cart, he moved off, not waiting to see if the bear would eat the piece of fruit. Beryl watched, hypnotised. She wanted Mrs Mary Plain to take her medicine, if it was medicine, but there was something shifty about the man — who was nothing like Greg really — and she wondered if it could be poison, a form of euthanasia. Why hadn't the zoo workers stayed to watch?

The black bear ambled toward the doctored fruit, nosing it hopefully. Then, just when Beryl was sure she would leave it alone, she juggled it into her mouth with a snaky tongue and swallowed, pointing her snout directly at the watching woman, but without a flicker of interest in her gluey eyes. She was all alone in the bear pit and had been alone for months now. Beryl stayed by the rail and watched, keeping the animal company while she digested her pill. 'Perhaps it's Prozac,' she said aloud.

'Antibiotic,' said a gritty voice behind her. It was the older zoo worker who had come back, on foot this time.

'Is she sick?'

'A bit poorly. She'll be right, we hope. With bears it's all about smell — did you know? Things have to smell right. We smell wrong to a bear.'

'What happened to her friend? Didn't she have a friend?'

'Not in my time. And she won't get one in my time. I've been given my cards, as they say in Brixton, where I come from.'

For a moment Beryl believed he had been told he was going to die, he looked so miserable. Then she thought again. 'You've been made redundant?'

He laughed. 'Hah! Is that what you call it? Three months they've given me. It should have been six, my solicitor told me. I've worked here for a good few years. Not worth the fuss to argue, not at my time of life. There's no one I have to support these days. I'm like her.' He pointed into the bear enclosure. 'Nothing smells right in my life. They say the Internet's how you do it these days.'

'Do what?' She looked blank.

'Look for a life partner. It isn't easy. I prefer the more direct approach myself.'

Beryl was alarmed. She took her hand off the rail.

'See what I mean? You're running away from me and I haven't even asked you yet. Don't run away.'

When Beryl left the zoo entrance and briskly retraced her steps she saw a figure at the edge of her vision, loitering outside her house. It was a woman with a green linen jacket and red hair. Clarice. Beryl stepped backwards like a startled horse. She didn't remember giving Clarice her address.

'Hi,' said Clarice. 'I was looking for you. Well — half . . .'

'Which half?' Beryl quipped, then ducked her head apologetically. It was a habit of hers to make semi-clever remarks when she was nervous, a habit Donald had derided, lengthening his top lip and wagging his head to signify affectionate boredom.

'I knew you lived in one of these houses from what you said.'

'But you guessed it was this one,' said Beryl, laying her hand on the gate. Her house was the only one in the street that hadn't been tarted up by new owners. 'You're right, it does need a bit of TLC.'

'It's a pretty house. I love it — from the outside anyway. We didn't see you the other night and I just wondered if you were all right.'

'I'm fine. Fine. I'm sorry I couldn't make it.' Her hand was still on the gate but she hadn't lifted the catch. 'Er. I'd ask you in for a cup of something, Clarice, but . . . it's not a good time. Actually we think there's a gas leak . . .'

'It's not supposed to smell these days, is it — natural gas?'

'Well no. Or it's different. Anyway we're keeping out of the kitchen till they get it sorted out.' She turned away and then turned back. 'But we could go for a coffee or something. There's a café along the road, if that . . . ?' She waited for Clarice's nod and then added, 'I'll just have to get my handbag. Won't be a minute.'

When they reached the café a paint-splattered stepladder blocked the entrance and the interior had been invaded by men in overalls wielding rollers.

'God, nothing stays the same for five minutes these days,' Clarice mourned.

'McDonald's does.'

'Oh — McDonald's.'

In fact when they walked on this was where they found themselves, in McDonald's, drinking coffee out of polystyrene cups. Warring siblings squealed in the red and yellow play area tunnels, climbing up and falling down with little legs flying.

'This is really disgusting, I'm sorry,' Beryl said.

'Yes it is. But at least it's hot — I can't stand lukewarm coffee. And it's nice to sit down. I've done quite a bit of walking this afternoon. I'm trying to walk off the party. Parties are bad for the health.'

'Oh yes. How was it?'

Clarice told Beryl about the flooded bathroom and the incensed downstairs owner. She made a joke of Una's despair when the man failed to stay for a drink. Men can be disappointing — you can only laugh. 'He won't be looking for you, will he? Your husband?'

'Greg? Oh, Greg's not my husband. He's — my friend.' She gave a shrug.

'Well, congratulations. I like to hear stuff like that. People think we oldies are past it. They ought to be told that we're just like the young, only older. Right?'

Beryl, instead of looking gratified, looked embarrassed. She buried her nose in her coffee, then began in a rush to tell Clarice about the sick bear in her cold stony space and the pink pill that should have been Prozac. She told her about the aging zoo worker and his redundancy. 'I think he might have been chatting me up — in fact I'm sure he was. Imagine. I mean, look at me.'

'What's wrong with you? You look quite nice and he obviously thought so.' Clarice laughed. 'Ironic, isn't it, how men always make advances to women who have no need because they've already got someone, thank you. It's like you send out a different kind of vibe; perhaps it's chemical. When I was married it was always happening. Whereas someone like Una at the moment — she's attractive, really she is — well, you met her — but she's desperate. She says she's desperate. That's bad.'

Beryl shifted uncomfortably on her seat. 'Perhaps you should send her down to the zoo then. This man — this Garth someone — he can't wait to meet somebody like your Una. He's not a bad-looking chap.' From behind, she added to herself. 'And he's kind to animals.' I think, she added but didn't say aloud. 'He must be, to work in that place. Mustn't he?'

'I might just do that.' Clarice looked into her empty mug and stood up. 'I'm getting another. One for you? Two of everything's good. My first husband used to say you need two wings to fly — although he was talking about whisky.' She didn't add that the whisky might have helped him fly from life, from her.

When Clarice had come back with the coffee Beryl thought she was beginning to understand why the woman needed that second wing. She wanted to talk about her friend Una.

'I really didn't know her that well when we decided to buy a place together. We did do it a bit fast but I still don't think it was a daft thing to do. On most levels it makes a lot of sense. The thing is I'm not sure she always tells me the truth about — well, anything really. It's a puzzle. This Sheree — is she her cousin or what? Una says one thing, Sheree says another. And Una doesn't tell me anything much about her husband, who's dead by the way. Some time ago, if you can believe what she says. It isn't that she tells lies — well, I don't know. Maybe she does tell lies sometimes. It's not what I'm used to. Perhaps I'm naïve but I'm used to believing what people tell me — I mean, people do tell the truth most of the time, don't they? Why bother to make stuff up? It would be a waste of time.'

'I suppose. How many months gone is she? This Sheree girl?' Beryl remembered the electric scream that had pierced the supermarket aisles.

'Four or five. I don't even know that.'

'So what is it that you mind most? That she doesn't tell you stuff? Or that she might tell lies?'

'The lies, to be honest.' Clarice snorted. 'Honest! Listen to me! But I can't stand dishonesty, it makes things so slippery and confused. I'm not just being moral about it. You know what I mean, don't you?'

Beryl nodded without speaking, then again more firmly. 'Of course. I can see it's a problem.' She lifted her wrist and studied her watch. 'You're probably right about Greg. He might be looking for me — I'd better go.' Then she suddenly blushed, a warm flood like one of those hot flushes she hoped she'd seen the last of, and had to reach down under her chair, taking a long time searching for her handbag.

'You said she didn't want to know me!' Beryl lifted her head up in the steamy kitchen, calling over her shoulder triumphantly to Greg, who was lounging in the living-room leather chair. She was making a big pot of beef stew to freeze in individual portions. She had enjoyed cooking for Donald, watching him dive in with his fork and give her a wink over the table sometimes if it was especially good. Now she cooked for the freezer, purchased on interest-free credit, and it gave her a different kind of pleasure, reminded her that she had moved with the times in some ways at least. 'She came looking for me specially.'

'Half looking,' Greg murmured in his nasal tones.

'Oh, that's just what she said.'

'And you said, "Go away, we've got a gas leak"!'

'I'm good at thinking fast when I have to.'

'We're keeping out of the kitchen — we! I thought you weren't going to talk to other people about me? And there you go, running off at the mouth, implying you've got a husband and he's called Greg.'

'I didn't. Not this time. I said you were my friend.'

'Not imaginary friend.'

'Of course not. I couldn't tell her that.'

'She told you she couldn't stand dishonesty. She thinks people tell the truth most of the time. She talks to you because you listen and you don't tell lies.'

'All right!' Beryl flung the Teflon serving spoon into the sink and bits of tomato gravy splattered the formica. 'I'm not perfect. But you aren't really a lie, are you? You can't be. You're something else. I don't know what to say to her!' She buried her face in a tea-towel and gave one dry sob before she blew her nose on the coarse linen.

'You sanctimonious pig!' she added.

Greg had followed her down the step into the kitchen and now said, more gently, 'I'm only kidding. You don't have to quote Abby at me. The TV series is over — gone — and she's gone with it. I'm your friend and you didn't lie, okay? Wipe your face and put that cloth in the washing basket. I'm just a little bit jealous.'

'Of Clarice? Jealous? That's ridiculous. What's Clarice got that you haven't? It's not a competition — you're completely different.'

'Exactly. She's real. Real people continue — they last forever.'

'They do not. They get old and they die. Or they simply go away.'

'And people remember them. When you're gone at least you'll have your name on a tombstone.'

Beryl found she had been playing with the soft skin on her hand, squeezing and pulping it so that the veins bulged like potato roots. Her hand was old and would get older. Greg was stuck in his late thirties. So? Late thirties was the age she felt inside herself. She returned to the task of ladling aromatic portions into plastic containers, but she was thinking about Clarice now and Greg slid away like a TV programme after the credits have floated up.

At the tram museum we had just missed the Fiducia ride. We walked in the vast, dusty shed among the exhibits: trams in varying states of repair, two-deckers and Palace trams, red with dashers in yellow and gold, three angled windows in the front and back. I heard myself and Una blurting small nostalgic utterances, to please Beryl as much as anything, although I did now vividly remember mornings crossing the city in a tram just like that one, as far as Bowen Street, where we'd had to transfer to a bus, sharing around my homework answers with the gigglers who occupied the back seats. It was for Beryl I'd suggested this outing up the coast. In Riddiford Street last week, contemplating a row of red buses, she had remembered the trams out loud — mournfully, I thought in retrospect — and mentioned that she'd known a conductor in those old days.

'Romantically?' I'd asked, inviting her to smile.

'Yes, I suppose so. That's about all.'

Sheree now walked ahead of us, not quite as if she had a bus to catch, but faster than we were strolling; obviously she didn't see the point of lingering as Beryl was doing. Staring.

*Beryl is on one of these trams while the driver in his big black coat operates the gears and makes the tram rattle along the tracks, seeming about to leave them at the corner but never quite doing so. Clang, and around they go. And the conductor is selling the tickets, clipping Beryl's. The sliding door into the front compartment bangs and bangs and there is a picture on it of the ivy-covered university building with soppy lines printed underneath.*

'Some poem or other,' Beryl muttered.

'Where?'

'On the glass door. Not here. It might be one of the others.'

Sheree had come back, removing the plug from her ear and letting it dangle on her spandex collar. 'Come on. We going to be here all day? What about that ice cream place?'

'I met my husband on a tram,' Beryl told me.

'How was that? Oh, you mean . . . ?'

'He was going to change my life.'

'I bet he did that.'

Beryl put her head down on her sleeve and began to

shake. Her chest creaked.

A startled glance from Una who then turned away, sauntering deliberately. She looked as if she was willing herself not to run. Sheree shrugged exaggeratedly, gave a clumsy skip, then walked to catch up with Una.

I touched Beryl's shoulder and she shuddered, raising her face, which had a string of saliva attaching her mouth to her sleeve. She shook her head and wiped moisture from the end of her nose, then patted me as if I was the one who needed comforting. It meant the spasm was over and she didn't want any questions about it please.

When we reached the other two Una administered a cheerful smile. 'Better now?' she breathed, like a hospital worker.

I wanted to hit her.

Later we bought Italian ice creams and dawdled on the beach as if nothing had happened. The sun had gone down and this stretch of sand was empty apart from two dog owners who stood chatting while their animals, one gangling and silent, one small and yappy, strained away from them. Dogs had to be kept on a lead, which was fine by me; I was nervous even around Marge's little slithery dachshund.

'I think I got an eyeful of your zoo bloke the other day,' Una said to Beryl over her mound of hokey pokey. 'Garth — wasn't that his name?'

'Did you go there?' I asked her. 'Really? You went to the zoo and you didn't tell me?' This pinged and resounded accusingly, an echo of something I might have said before. 'You laughed at me when I suggested it!'

'I laughed because you didn't expect me to take you seriously. Anyway, I thought I might just check the place out. There's more than one animal in a zoo, you know. I might have come back engaged to the keeper.'

'But you thought you saw this Garth?'

'Well, he was balding, definitely getting on a bit. He and another chap were doing something with the giraffes — feeding them I suppose. I like the giraffes but I didn't hang about.'

'Well, why not? After all that?'

'All what? I was only there five minutes, after my dentist — his rooms are nearby. I wasn't too struck by the look of your Garth. He was frowning.'

'Frowning at you?'

'I don't believe he saw me actually. Anyway I'm not desperate.'

Beryl and I glanced at each other, disbelieving, and then quickly away again.

'I'll give him your phone number, shall I?' Beryl asked, then looked surprised at the sound of her own voice, strong and normal. The rum and raisin in a waffle cone must have refreshed her and wiped away her earlier mood.

'Oh, don't be so silly!' Una snorted. Then — 'Will you really? What will you say?'

I couldn't help smiling at the speed of this U-turn.

Beryl was surprised too. 'What do you want me to say?'

'Goes like this: 'I know this very nice lady who's got a window' — isn't that what people say these days . . . ?'

'A window?' Beryl sounded puzzled.

'I think that's a great idea,' I offered. 'You know this nice woman who's a lot of fun. Okay, Una?'

'I'm sure he'd prefer you to me,' Beryl said, sounding less sure of herself. 'I don't really want to talk to the man again, but I will if you want me to.' She drew up her shoulders. 'All right.'

Sheree, who had wandered off kicking at driftwood in time to whatever music her ears were drinking in, was back now. She frowned as if she thought we had bad news to impart but all Beryl said when the girl removed an earplug was: 'So when's the baby due, Sheree?'

'Good question. I can't bloody wait!'

'Yes — it must be exciting. I wouldn't be able to wait either.'

Sheree stared at Beryl's expression, puzzling. 'No — I just want it out, that's all. My bum's big enough without having a bum in the front as well. I want rid.'

'Oh, it's more than that! It's a life!' Beryl was clearly shocked. 'It's just happened sooner than you wanted, I expect . . .'

Una leaned forward. 'Leave it, Beryl. It's not worth wasting your puff.'

I sat across from Beryl in the new Polynesian restaurant that boasted 'competitive' prices, eating kumara chips and noticing that Beryl was wearing lipstick. Una had said, 'I know she doesn't like me much but you could have asked her here if she can't cope with entertaining in her own home. Why is that, do you think?'

I told her I thought Beryl must be ashamed. 'Her place is pretty grim outside and God knows what horrors there might be inside.' I'd remembered the gas leak. The house clearly needed money spent on it and Beryl cared. I explained she must have been barely keeping herself afloat on her income, whatever that was, probably some income-tested benefit — well, you could tell from the clothes she wore — flannel shirts and glittery cotton things that had been hanging in a wardrobe for thirty years or more. 'Or it could be that friend of hers. I know he doesn't like parties.'

'Perhaps he's fat and toothless,' Una had said happily. 'Yeah — it would be just like a man not to notice the price of meat or how much toilet paper he goes through. Men can't even shit straight.'

'You're right. I bet that's it — she's just the type to get exploited by a bloke.'

Una frowned. 'You're not trying to say something about me, are you? I think I pay my whack.'

'No, no, of course you do. I'm not suggesting anything.' I'd temporarily forgotten that Una was in one of her glooms.

Now I sat across from Beryl and saw that as well as the lipstick she had had a decent haircut: it appeared to have given her the courage to talk about her Donald's desertion twenty-six years ago. Twenty-six! I couldn't help being surprised that the woman was still hurting. Surely other stuff had happened to her since then.

'I'm like you, I suppose,' Beryl said. 'I tend to believe people, specially when I've asked them particularly to be honest with me.' It was comforting to find she remembered our earlier conversation, not like Una. 'I did wonder about Donald that summer — he'd been so quiet and I'd noticed, even though I'm quiet myself, or I used to be. And sometimes he smelled different when he kissed me goodnight. I remember thinking — that's funny, you get this definite odour when you're grumpy with me, a kind of chemical smell, like talcum powder. I thought it must be some hormonal thing. Then I thought no, it smells a bit like perfume. So I wound myself up and I asked him — Are you having an affair? Tell me the truth, I said. The truth is important to me.'

I leaned forward with my forkful of lamb shank hovering expectantly. 'And he said?'

'He said no, he wasn't. I was so relieved!'

'But he was.'

'Yes, he was. And he had to tell me in the end, before he packed up and left me, so it was a waste of all that putting on an act. Stupid man.'

'Oh dear.'

'Your second husband didn't do anything like that?'

'Not exactly. Nor my first husband, David. He just died. Dying's worse.'

'I don't know. Oh, I'm sorry, of course it must be.'

'But you've got Greg. As a matter of fact I did wonder for a moment if he'd let you come out for a girls' dinner. He didn't like the idea of our party, did he?'

Beryl looked flustered. 'It wasn't quite like that. He's not a bully. I feel I should consider him, that's all — take his wishes into account.'

I looked deliberately sceptical.

'What about your downstairs tenant?' Beryl changed the subject. 'Was there any real damage to his bathroom ceiling?'

'Owner,' I corrected. 'We own shares. No. I think we pretty much got away with that. But we're grateful he noticed — drew our attention to it. I might have gone on sleeping.' I worried my rice with my fork, stirring it but not attempting to eat any more of it. 'Kevin, his name is. What did I tell you about him?'

'Nothing much. Just that Una wanted to meet him but he didn't seem keen.'

'That's right. She even went again after we'd checked out his ceiling, and asked him up for a drink, but he was too busy — or said he was. She got in a bit of a state as it happens — went into one of her paranoia phases. "I'm a worthless, ugly slut" sort of thing. She decided after that that Marge hates her too and avoids the lift in case she runs into her. And the dog — India she's called — doesn't like her either. Una says. She thinks it's because she must smell bad to dogs — I mean evil bad, not stinky.'

'Oh my God. Poor woman.'

'Is she? Yes, I suppose she is. And the worst thing is that I ran into Kevin in Courtenay Place and he asked me to have a drink with him in a wine bar — a champagne place around the corner in Blair Street. Rather nice. I've always wanted to try it.'

'Well, what's wrong with that?'

'I could hardly go, could I? With Una feeling all that?'

'You didn't go?'

'No. Not this time anyway.' I gave a little smile because she seemed worried for me. 'That's why I really hope something comes of this Garth idea — at the zoo? I don't suppose you talked to him?'

Beryl looked at once pleased with herself. She sat up straighter and dropped a glob of chutney on her blouse without noticing. 'I wondered when you were going to ask me that. I did! I did. I had to search for him all over but I found him. He looked a bit blank at first but then I could see he was interested. I just shoved it at him — the number on the back of a piece of card so he wouldn't lose it easily. And I took off.' She chuckled.

I couldn't believe she'd really done it. Good on her. I leaned forward with my table napkin and removed the chutney. 'That's great.'

'If he rings up you might answer the phone,' Beryl thought aloud. 'Perhaps you'd like to meet him yourself?'

'Me? Christ, no. I don't want a depressed, desperate man. He and Una sound made for each other.' I hoped I wasn't talking bullshit.

While Beryl studied the dessert menu I listened to the serious CD track that was playing over the speakers and wondered if I sounded frivolous and careless. No — if I were these things I'd be sitting in a champagne bar with Kevin instead of in this quiet, old-lady place, waiting for bread pudding.

Two days later Una and Garth had an assignation at The Jimmy, the bar below the restored St James Theatre. She spent an hour in the bathroom, then disappeared into her bedroom for even longer. The clock was ticking and she was cutting it fine. I thought she might have lost her nerve and sunk into one of her self-destructive moods which were as vicious as razors tearing at arms and wrists; I was about to barge in to offer support when she emerged. She had done something to her plump face so that the dark discoloration on her cheekbones and in the corner of her mouth was painted out and her lips glistened rather stickily.

'Wow.' I had nothing more to say after this.

'Bloody contacts. I was fighting for ages to get them in comfortably — reckon I need new ones. They're harder to wear as you get past forty. So I look okay then?'

'You know you do. Fantastic. I haven't seen that top before.'

'New. I did a bit of retail therapy last week — just as well. Okay — shit! Look at the time!'

When Una had gone, heels clacking in the thinly carpeted foyer, I had the place to myself, unusually. I poured a large glass of grapefruit juice and sat in the last strip of sunlight that draped no wider than a scarf on the high back of the burgundy armchair. What if Una came home weeping, having been physically assaulted by a homicidal psychopath, her new black satin top ripped, all the little yellow buttons stripped off like popcorn, her sticky lipstick smeared ear to ear? Not very likely. Una could look after herself. I recalled the surprising muscles in those arms when she was cleaning up the flooded bathroom. No, Una would be fine. She might get drunk.

She might . . . And from there I climbed onto a different train of thought. Una and Garth became an item, serious stuff. They made plans for their future, the schmaltzy wedding at Old St Paul's, the combining of assets. If he had any assets. And where would that leave me? Would I mind, feel abandoned? That was daft. If those two got it together perhaps they'd offer me her share of the apartment, which wouldn't be a very bad thing — but no, I couldn't afford to buy her out, no way. Damn. Every decision, every life variation as you got older involved money and financial survival was so precarious. Was it always like this? When I was young my parents or their friends hadn't seemed to agonise about their financial options in quite this way. Old age used to mean you had more, not less, a mortgage-free home at last, perhaps a holiday bach at the beach and things, rooms full of things, not just pot pourri and bric-a-brac like my Lavabo sign, my burgundy armchair and bookcases, the framed prints. What had I done with all my income over the years?

The hospital and then the lodge had gobbled most of my mother's remaining money after the funeral expense, so there had been very little to inherit; and of course divorce was expensive, but these days nearly everyone went through one. They must just hide it better. Well, I could rent out the other rooms to a boarder — someone easy-going who worked longer hours than me — and pay that rent to Una, providing of course she agreed to this arrangement. I heard myself sigh, took too large a gulp of grapefruit juice and choked on it. 'Silly bitch!' I coughed. There I went again, getting way ahead of myself and now trying to choke myself. Just as well I could laugh. But hadn't Mama Cass been alone and laughing when she died choking on a ham sandwich? Bloody hell, Saturday used to be a day for fun and relaxation. 'So what do you call this if not relaxation?' I said aloud.

Sheree's key jiggled in the lock in time to catch the end of this. She had her Walkman on so might not have heard me talking to myself but she did cast me a curious grimace, bumping deliberately into the armchair on her way to the back bedroom, almost as if she considered that particular chair was hers and had been wrongfully claimed.

Two minutes in her bedroom and the girl was back, rocking on rubber heels.

'Aren't you going anywhere?' she asked me, shoving her chin out.

'Not tonight, sorry. Why? What have you got planned?'

'Me? I don't make plans. I just go with the flow.'

'Come on, Sheree. I'm not silly. Is there some friend you want to invite back here? I wouldn't blame you. You're allowed, you know, within reason. I don't — *we* don't want you dealing drugs or putting yourself at risk, but you must need some company of your own age. Eh? What about that girl — Jilly?'

'Jilly vanilla?'

'Who?'

'She's a weak-arse bitch.' Sheree twirled a dining-room chair on one leg without explaining but I imagined I felt a slight easing of tension in the girl. The cane bottom tipped out of the chair and she reached clumsily to restore it.

I helped her with this. 'There's lasagne in the fridge to be heated up. I'm not hungry yet but you know how to use the microwave. All right?'

'I don't do drugs,' Sheree asserted suddenly with some force.

'No, I didn't think you did. It would be thoughtless while you're carrying someone's baby, you know that.'

'Someone,' she repeated with a low giggle. 'So you believe I'm going to give it away, do you?'

'Of course. Aren't you? But I didn't mean that. It must have a father out there somewhere, that's all I meant.'

'Tyler. I told you. But he's not out there any more. They made sure of that. He said it would happen — he was waiting for it to happen but I didn't believe him. He was only fourteen, younger than me.'

'Fourteen? Is that for real, Sheree? The father was only fourteen years old?'

'Don't keep saying that! The father! It sounds so mad when I think of Tyler — it sounds like you're making fun of him.'

'So what happened? Did he get put in some remand home, or what?' And how was he connected to Una? Was it Tyler who was the cousin and Sheree simply the girlfriend?

Sheree coughed a hard laugh into the juicy fingers of her hand. 'I wish! He'd get out of a home, wouldn't he? You don't usually get out of a coffin, specially once it goes up in smoke.'

'No! Oh Sheree, that's awful. Why didn't Una tell me?' Then I narrowed my eyes. Was I doing it again, believing everything I was told, just like poor Beryl whose husband reeked of perfume? I decided to change tack and said in a more neutral tone, 'You didn't want an abortion or you'd have had one, I expect.'

'I'd have got rid of it if I could, yeah, but they wouldn't let me, said I was too late. I got my dates wrong. How was I to know what was going on? I wasn't living here — I was in Sydney.' As if that might have explained any discrepancy in her story. She looked across at me and must have seen the doubts jostling behind my eyes because she became defensive suddenly, her face closed like a door shutting and she muttered. 'Why am I talking to you? You don't want to know.'

I assumed a neutral expression, then tried to upgrade it to sympathy. I did in fact feel some sympathy for the position Sheree was in, pregnant at sixteen, never mind how. The girl could be behaving far worse: she could be drinking Una's vodka or stealing the silver to score heroin and damage her unborn child. Not that she'd get much for my old spoons and forks and the little silver table tennis cup Una had received while at school. 'I do want to hear.'

''Cos you're nosy. But you don't believe it.' Sheree had moved closer to the armchair until she was standing beside my left ear and leaned in almost threateningly. Too close. I refused to turn my head. If this was to be another performance like the screaming exercise in the supermarket . . . 'I can scream too,' I began to say. And then I very nearly did scream. There was a metallic click inside Sheree's fat hand and a knife blade cut the air, a fine, silver point, pricking my neck.

'Sheree! What *is* that? Put it away!'

'Flick knife. Got it in Sydney. Keep it in my shoe — not while I was on the plane, they'd have nicked it.'

'That's an illegal weapon. Do put it away.'

'What's a legal weapon when it's at home? I'm illegal. It's illegal to have sex before you're sixteen.'

'You were both illegal — it takes two to make a baby. Why do you want a weapon anyway? What are you defending yourself against?'

'You don't know much, do you? People get killed in broad daylight. Innocent people. All sorts are out to get you.'

'Wellington's hardly New York.'

'What about that guy in the lift shaft down Courtenay Place? And that woman . . . Una told me about that.'

'I don't know why she'd talk to you about such stuff.'

'She wants me to be scared, eh? She's pissed off that Tyler got done and not me, but he was asking for it.'

'If she wants you to be scared it's for your own good, I'm sure,' I said, sounding less than sure. 'She wouldn't want you carrying a knife. Don't put it back in your shoe. Put it in your bedroom if you need to keep it. I'm going to heat up our dinner.'

It wasn't until the microwave had pinged and we were sitting with the cheesy lasagne lolling below our forks that I asked the question, and not for the first time. 'So tell me about Tyler. What relation was he to Una? Was he her cousin?'

'No.' Sheree shovelled pasta greedily. 'Grandson, what else? This —' she patted her tummy, 'this'll be a great-grandchild. Wicked, eh? I don't suppose she wants to know that.'

The movie on Prime was just finishing when Una let herself back into the apartment, bringing with her scents of stale cigarette smoke and the liquid soap they dispense in ladies' toilets. Her Estée Lauder Pleasures had gone stuffy on her skin. Flinging herself wearily onto one of the cane chairs, she pronounced, in answer to my raised eyebrows, 'Nah. Not really.'

'Not really what?'

'Not really my kind of bloke.'

'Oh. That's a shame. So you're not going to see him again?'

'I didn't say that. Probably a drink after work on Tuesday. I need to look in my diary.'

'Oh yes.' I gave her my sceptical smile. 'Tuesdays are often busy, eh?'

'Is she in bed?'

'Sheree? I think so. The movie was a bit heavy for her.' I wondered briefly how much to tell her about the flick-knife episode or Sheree's disclosure and decided not to say anything at all. If Una could be secretive so could I. I finished stacking the dishwasher, frowning to keep my secrets locked in, while Una was occupying the bathroom.

'What's up?' Una approached at last, her face scrubbed red around her nostrils, eyes pink and piggy, denuded of kohl and eyeshadow. 'Something wrong with the dishwasher?'

'How do you mean? It's fine — why?'

'You looked like you'd gone into a trance. I suppose you had a boring night in but you can't blame me for that. Good blokes don't just come to the door and ask you for a glass of water — you have to go looking. Pull out some stops.'

'I'm perfectly okay. I had a nice night in, thank you. And Sheree was quite good company.'

'You're kidding! She shared her Walkman with you, did she?'

'We talked. About the baby and stuff.'

'Oh.' Una tugged her dressing gown about her. 'Oh. Well, you'll need a good night's sleep then. I know I do. See you in the morning — ta ta.'

# Beryl

Beryl liked to think her tired old house was at least spotless. There had been a mouse in the kitchen, years before, quickly banished with a few green pellets that had turned him into a foul smell behind the fridge. After that she had blocked up his means of access. The kitchen smelled sweet enough now, with window pots of rosemary, and basil in season. In the entrance hallway there was a shallow pottery bowl of pot pourri which had lost most of its smell. It sat on a low wooden chest with round feet, next to a spindly table, hand painted with twining plants and multicoloured berries. This last was something brought with her as part of a trousseau from her parents' house in a nearby street. After they passed away — both of them relatively young by today's standards — she had acquired other items to decorate her and Donald's home — a set of silver-plated candlesticks with fluted purple glass to hold the stems of wax, a wooden-handled parasol with a painted island scene that billowed above her bedroom doorway accumulating dust. In the living room beside the tiled fireplace, converted to hold bookshelves, a prim set of brass-handled poker, shovel and hearth brush stood uselessly at the ready, as did the set of bellows on the grate.

Beryl's vacuum cleaner was old but it worked, or at least it made an impressive noise. The dark grey living-room carpet was becoming difficult, clinging onto pieces of hair and other dropped fibres so that she ended up doing the final clean on her bony knees, using her fingers to pluck up recalcitrant fluff and stuff it into the nozzle. She felt a kind of relationship with the machine, which had aged like her and was also losing some of its power, although not enough to make a fuss about. Her friendship with Clarice was causing her to look at her home through new eyes and she was surprised to feel the remnants of domestic pride stirring. She had gone to some trouble when she was first married, promising herself visitors and family gatherings that never quite came about. She had even picked up a paintbrush and wielded it herself while Donald was working. All that had come to a swift end in 1976, after his departure. Looking about her she could see not one item of decoration that she had acquired since that time, unless you called kitchen pots and paraphernalia decorative. The purple colander that protected her sink waste was trying hard but she considered it an ugly thing. And there were certainly plenty of new — or second-hand

— books furnishing her shelves with colour. It was a shame. The place was really asking for visitors.

'That's right,' Greg murmured through his nose. 'You'll have to get rid of me somehow. It's not really a problem. You could tell her I'm away or I've walked out on you. Easy. That's what a normal person would say.'

'But you haven't.'

'That's beside the point. She wouldn't see me even if I was sitting right beside her. So?'

'I'm a lousy liar. I'd muck it up. Liars have to believe what they say when they say it.'

'Don't worry — you'll lie when you have to, and you'll make a fair job of it. Everyone does it. Look at your Donald. He didn't want to hurt you.'

'Donald? Hurt himself, more like. It was himself he was looking after.'

'And who are you looking after? You just want to feel good about yourself, that's all.'

Was that all? Maybe Beryl feared asking Clarice into her home because Greg might distract her deliberately, might trick her into appearing weird and, yes, nuts. She was no more nuts than she had been as a four-year-old who played with an imaginary dog, whistling for and patting him and feeding him her crusts under the table, but Clarice would see it differently perhaps. She wouldn't understand that Greg had been a part of her daily life for so long now that denying him would be something like going out in public without her knickers and bra. Plenty of women had done that in the seventies and survived, but Beryl had not been one of them; and even Germaine Greer had changed her tune since then. 'I bet she's wearing knickers to keep her warm today.'

'Germaine?'

'That's right. You understand me so well,' Beryl said.

*T*hree days a week I finished work at two o'clock and relished arriving home before Una. That Wednesday I was walking across the foyer from the lift wondering if Sheree would be ensconced in my armchair watching the Australian soaps, when I heard a man's footsteps bounding up the stairs. I don't know who I thought it might be — unlikely that it was Kevin who lived on the ground floor — but I lost the rhythm of my progress, tripped on the edge of the raised tiling and ended up sitting down, reaching for my shoulder bag that had fallen open, pushing my heel back into my sandal. Then I looked up. Not Kevin but a stranger with greying hair straggled from the northerly and exposing a dented bald patch.

'Hello. All right? You must be . . . ?' Whatever he was beginning to say fizzled to a stop as he took in the look on my face, which was probably less than friendly.

'I expect Una's not home yet. It's just — I've got a park outside which is a bit of luck, so I thought I'd toddle up and see if there was anyone to let me in. I'm Garth, by the way. I've got a load of meat for you in the car. For the two of you,' he added, smiling energetically so that his moustache moved. He held out his hand as if he expected me to shake it.

'Meat,' I repeated stupidly, keeping my own hand firmly on the handle of my shoulder bag.

'Didn't she say? I told her I'd got a full freezer. Had a bit of luck in the pub on Saturday. You know they come round with these raffles? I can't stop winning — I'll have to give up my beer. It's too much meat for me, I'm not much of a cook. I'll bring it up, shall I? She said there'd be freezer space.'

'Ah. Sorry. I've just had a bit of a day.' I stepped ahead of Garth and had the usual difficulty struggling with the key before it decided to turn in the lock. He stood watching this operation with an eager, almost greedy look on his face that made me feel uncomfortable. It was over a week since Una's date with him at The Jimmy and it sounded as if they were seeing more of each other than I'd been aware of. Whatever had happened to female confidences? When we were inside Sheree wagged a hand at me, which was encouraging behaviour. I wagged back, then turned to Garth, who was peering with obvious curiosity, flickering his pale eyes over the walls, the kitchen appliances, for all the world like a prospective buyer in the hands of an estate agent.

'But you haven't fetched your meat yet,' I reminded him and a sudden chill clamped a cold hand on my stomach. Why wasn't Una here? Come on Una, where are you? I'd remembered Sheree's warnings. 'You don't know much, do you? People get killed. Innocent people.' For the moment I was glad of Sheree and her flick knife.

'Of course. I'll be right back.'

'Who's he?' Sheree wanted to know. 'Is he your bloke?'

'Una's, not mine.'

'Oh yeah. Boring. What do you do with a man when you're that old? Ballroom dancing?'

'He's got some meat for us. He won it in a raffle. What time is it?'

Sheree waved at the clock on the stove. 'What's up?'

'I'm wondering when Una will be back.'

'Scared he's going to make a move on you? She'd kill you. Or him.'

'I wish you wouldn't go on about killing all the time. We're not all homicidal maniacs.'

We could hear Garth wheezing in the doorway: he might have been carrying a body and not simply two parcels in supermarket bags. They were large packages, however, and wrapped in clear plastic so that in one bag the blood showed red on slabs of steak with white flashes of bone and in the other something — perhaps chicken — bulged white lardy flesh, a bit like Garth's advancing forehead.

'Eugh!' I looked at all this sprawled on the kitchen

bench and was reluctant to handle it.

'I know. I'd unwrapped the stuff trying to fit it in my own freezer so it's done up a bit amateurishly, but it's in smaller packs so it's more convenient for you.'

Sheree had roused herself to come closer, her eyes on stalks, and when he had finished speaking she reached down and pulled open the freezer door with a flourish.

'Thanks.' I introduced the girl, then said, 'You could start stacking this stuff for me while I make Garth a cup of tea. Would you mind?'

'Tea! I bet he doesn't drink tea.'

'I do actually. Just an ordinary gumboot does me fine. But I'm on a thirty-minute park, so I'll toddle off. I'll phone Una some time this evening.'


Una scanned the freezer contents with amazement. She appeared startled that Garth had been in her home while she wasn't there.

'But you knew about the meat.'

'Oh, he muttered something the other day but I thought it was an excuse to get himself asked to dinner. I didn't even give him this address. Oh yes, I did — more or less. He must have been hanging about, checking us out. Creepy.'

'He certainly gave me the creeps. I don't fancy cooking any of that meat — I kept thinking of Sweeney Todd.'

'Oh, come on! He's not a bad bloke really, just a bit sad. I suppose I should ask him to dinner. I'm sure the meat's fine.'

'No! Please. You can do what you like with him in private. This is my home too.'

For a moment the air between us crackled. Una's head was lowered, like an animal ready to butt its way out of trouble. Then she said, 'So I can bring him home and fuck him in my bedroom with the door shut — is that how the rules go?'

I laughed, but uneasily. 'Well yes, if that's what you want. I'm not being unreasonable here. I don't like having things sprung on me. Everything we do together needs negotiating, that's all I'm saying.'

'Christ. Might as well be married.'

'I thought you enjoyed being married — or was that just another story?'

Una puffed air impatiently from nostrils that still wore a layer of Estée Lauder and strode off to her bedroom.

I had spent thirty years in charge of my own steering wheel before I sold my car and became demoted to passenger; my own decision of course. I sat in the front seat of Una's Mazda, watching her negotiate the hillside bends to Makara, steadying a potted chrysanthemum for David between my knees. I was wearing jeans that day instead of my usual cross-cut skirt, drawing a comment from Sheree: 'Shit. My gran gave up jeans when she was forty.' And the answering comment from Una: 'I expect your gran was fat.' The hills were green and buttery with untidy gorse, the road littered in places with cheesy crumbles of clay following the rain-drenched weekend. I'd felt touched when Una suggested this outing, particularly as she had been clearly wounded by my rejection of her dinner party idea. I saw this journey to visit the graves of our respective husbands as a peace offering and a thoughtful one. 'I've brought a couple of cloths to clean the bird shit off the headstones — one for you. There's a tap.'

'Of course. How often do you visit?'

'Not often. I know he's not really there.' I said this firmly enough, but the closer the Mazda hummed toward the cemetery gates the less I believed it and caught myself preparing speeches under my breath to deliver to his headstone. The car swooped up between patterns of well-shaved lawn, past the Jewish section and the Chinese, to the interdenominational area. The trees had grown tall since the interment ceremony, a surprising number of years ago now, and I enjoyed the fact that David would approve: he had impressed on Stuart and Sophie the importance of trees.

'Where is he? I mean, the grave?' Una asked and waited for me to wave the hand that wasn't burdened with the chrysanthemum. She retrieved her own spray of red silk roses from the back seat.

'Your Roy must be closer to the road,' I guessed, remembering the death was more recent. 'Can I see?'

'Actually he's over in the Catholic section. I'll leave you to it. See you back here at the car in — twenty minutes?'

There was a regulation height for headstones in this wide new cemetery, which made for a crude conformity. I stepped politely along the rows of narrow tombs, taking care not to stumble on the private thoughts of sleeping identities — a bit like airline travel. It dislodged a distant holiday memory I'd shared with David. It wasn't that I believed exactly, but rather that I couldn't quite disbelieve the cemetery stories told to me by my grandmother. Never speak ill of the dead. Never tread on the top end of buried coffins. At six I'd thought skeletal arms might reach out for my feet; at fifty-nine I told myself it was about respect. Grandma rested in the old Karori cemetery, the real one, with my mother and father, not in this new settlement.

David's grave was one of the end ones in his row, cosily guarded by a swathe of shrubbery. The birds had had a fair old time trying to obliterate the white letters carved in shiny grey granite. I arranged my pot of yellow blooms and began to scrub busily with the cloth, telling David just what I thought of my new housemate but keeping it light. I didn't like to think of him worrying on my behalf when he should be resting in peace. But he couldn't worry, could he? Not if he was in heaven, that worry-free paradise where he should be, supposing there was such a thing as an afterlife. I had a taste for Hollywood afterlife movies. *Truly Madly Deeply* I'd seen four times.

'If Una doesn't want me to see her Roy's headstone, I'm not going to bring her here to see yours — why should I? I didn't even know he was a Catholic — she tells me so little. Should I mind? I want to tell her my things — I need to spill over at somebody. But never mind. We've got a nice apartment — you'd hate it, but I like being so central, just a short walk to Courtenay Place. And the kids are doing well, but you'll know that. Stuart's in love again and Sophie's happy with her engineer — or at least I think so. Maybe nobody tells me

the truth any more. No grandchildren yet. Oh dear.'
I didn't usually cry at David's headstone — or hadn't for
years. Una was supposed to be the depressive one, not
me. I certainly wasn't crying because I was missing grandchildren, although it might have sounded like that.
I laughed and sniffed, ransacking my handbag for a tissue
to wipe my eyes, and corrected this wrong impression for
the man who was lying beside me, six feet under. 'I don't
want grandchildren — or not in a rush — I just want to
be able to believe the people I care about. It used to be
easier, or else I was just thick. I'm starting to question
everything I hear. I was even suspicious of Una's pathetic
boyfriend. I guess that's what it's like, being alive. You're
right — I'm lucky to be alive.'

Una was waving from the car, using the cloth I'd given
her as a flag. Then she climbed in and drooped in the
driver's seat, watching my careful progress through the
tombstones, so that by the time I arrived the ignition was
already switched on and the engine idling impatiently.

'Okay?' Una asked but it was hardly a question.
'Let's get out of this place. You can't help thinking, can
you? We're next.'

We travelled as far as Karori where the narrow road
met the bus route, without exchanging more than a few
words. Then Una said, with another sideways look, 'I
think you've been crying.' She sounded impressed as if
I'd performed appropriately and convincingly whereas
she had acted like a badly schooled film extra. No tears,
only a sombre face. 'How many years ago was it? You
did tell me.'

'Nineteen eighty. Muldoon days.'

'Was he interested in politics then?'

'Not specially, but Muldoon was on the news that day, I remember — we'd been watching it and then . . . What about Roy? Had he been ill?'

'We were never as close as you two were, from what you've told me. He sounds like some kind of saint, your hubby. That's what widows do, though, isn't it? Goes like this: sanctify the dear departed or they won't spit on you in hell. I'm not saying you do. Or me of course. But people do say that.'

I felt anger welling. I didn't believe for a moment that Una didn't classify me with all those other fawning widows. A question surged in my gorge and before I could help myself forced itself out between my clenched teeth. 'So what would Roy have thought about your great-grandchild, do you suppose?'

'My . . . ?'

'Sheree's baby.'

The car slewed to the side of the road and parked sharply and clumsily. I threw Una a startled look; when she didn't speak but only stared at the steering wheel, I wondered if I was expected to get out and take a bus.

'Is that what she's been saying?'

'Well — yes. She said Tyler was your grandson and he's the father. Isn't it true?'

'Okay — well now you know. She did promise not to say.'

'You can't have expected to keep it from me. She's only a kid and we live in the same flat. Anyway why, for goodness' sake? Don't you want to have a great-grandchild?'

'She's not going to keep it so there's really not a lot of point, is there? Not a lot to celebrate.' She had kept her head half turned away, watching the passing cars and now a group of Marsden schoolgirls jostling and calling to one another, tossing a chocolate bar like a netball. She turned back and looked into my face. 'There was no reason to tell you: it's not your problem. I know she's a cow to live with but she'll leave in a few months and we can get on with our lives.'

'I suppose —' I began then stopped. I was puzzled.

'Suppose what?'

'I suppose it's pretty good of you, having her, under the circumstances. You didn't have to.'

'Yeah.' Una was pleased at this. 'I don't know why I did, actually. A weak moment — I have those, believe it or not. It was my daughter's idea, as a matter of fact, she got me to promise. She can be quite bossy, my Jane, even long distance.'

'Where is she?'

'America. Phoenix.' She reached for the ignition and the car was in motion again. 'She won't come home. She's got better things to do with her life — worthy things. Improving herself, and everybody else that comes into her orbit. Deluded, but worthy. What am I saying? It's a lot of crap actually, but she believes different.'

'Are you sure she wants Sheree to give the baby away?'

Una shrugged.

'Couldn't she decide to bring up the baby herself? I know I'd want to if it was me. And she says Tyler was murdered. Can that be true?'

We were at the traffic lights; the car jerked forward and narrowly avoided bumping into a stationary Toyota in front.

Una said, 'If you don't want me to have an accident, I suggest you stop talking about this. Now. All right?'

*F*ourteen-year-old Tyler *had to press his hands deep in his jeans pockets to stop them shaking. He said it was the coke that made them shake but Sheree guessed it was the business with the gun in Colombia. The boss guy had lent him a gun, an eight to start with, but then he'd been given his own tool, a heavy thing he had to hold up with both hands and use his middle finger for the trigger. Aim for the back of the head, he'd been told, so that's how he did it, with his eyes half shut. When the man went down Tyler had pissed himself with surprise, he told Sheree. Four hundred dollars for using his finger. And you get it for free! He was pleased with himself until he started to have the dreams — dreams that the man he killed came back and pulled his ears. 'Why would he pull your ears?' Sheree had wanted to know.*

*'I hate anyone touching my ears, I've never told*

*anyone that. He must be a real ghost to know that about me.'*

*'It's a dream, Ty. You're in Sydney now.'*

*'But he can send people to get me. That's what the dead man's pulling my ears to tell me. Mum says you pay for being a bad spirit. I'm bad, eh? You're sleeping with someone who's going to be dead!'*

*'I'm not sleeping. You won't let me sleep.'*

I turned on the kitchen light to reveal Sheree with a teaspoon plunged in the peanut butter jar. 'What are you doing in the dark?'

'Eating peanut butter.' Her speech was thick with it.

'I can see that.'

'It helps me sleep.'

'I'm going to make some hot milk. Do you want some? With Milo?'

'Might as well. Ta. What have you got to keep you from sleeping? Oh that's right, old people don't need to sleep, do they?'

'Who says I'm old?'

'Fifty-nine you said.'

'And you remembered.'

'Why wouldn't I? It's old people forget. Old people are lucky.' She screwed the lid on the peanut butter jar and reached past me to replace it in the cupboard. This looked like an improvement on her earlier habits.

I shut the microwave door on two mugs of milk and pressed Quickstart several times. 'That's a stupid thing to say.' Only someone as young as Sheree could say that so carelessly. 'When you get to my age you'll know how stupid that is. Memory's a precious thing.'

'Hah! Depends what you got in your head, eh?'

I narrowed my eyes. 'Something you want to forget?'

'Mind your own.'

Two mugs of milk juddered chocolate froth as we bumped elbows on our way to claim the burgundy armchair. I reached it first and Sheree had to make do with the cane sofa. She was wearing a grey men's singlet that hugged her distorted belly button and drooped low on one side. I noticed that her big toes jutted out prominently and the nails needed clipping. I resisted the impulse to tell her so and reach for the sideboard drawer where scissors lay in wait. Sheree was not my child and didn't want to be treated as such. Or maybe she did and that was why she was still in the main room. She sat, head bowed, slurping at the yellow mug, wriggling her bare toes and looking everywhere but at me.

'You want to talk about something?' I asked.

'Like what?'

'The baby?'

Sheree answered by placing her long-toed feet on the carpet and pulling herself up from the cane seat. The baby was growing heavier. 'See you in the morning.'

'Right.' I squashed my chin and squinted to examine my dressing gown collar for spilled Milo. And then I was on my own again.

I remembered why I'd been having trouble sleeping. There had been a peculiar message for Una on the answerphone but it wasn't from Garth this time, it was from someone who called himself Roy and claimed to be — 'Your ex. Remember?' But the husband, Roy, was dead — wasn't he? — and buried in the Catholic section of Makara cemetery.

It wasn't that I believed it was a ghost speaking. On the contrary, I believed he was a real person, with that complaining, gravelly voice, but I was horridly embarrassed by this blatant evidence of Una's mendacity. If I drew Una's attention to the call she'd be angry — she'd flip out and the anger would, perversely, be directed at *me*, I felt sure of that. Oh shit. And before I could think any further I'd plopped my finger down and wiped the message — it had seemed the easiest thing to do. I could have left it there for Una to pick up and deal with in her own way, but too late, I'd done it, and now the message was lodged in my brain like a headache. What was it Sheree had said? 'Depends what you've got in your head.' I wanted to abolish this memory, for the time being anyway. Damn Una for lying. But that was no reason for me to be dishonest or at least keep the truth away from her. This Roy had wanted something of his wife, something she had taken with her when she 'bloody walked out'. It could have been important. I would have to confess at some stage. We'd eaten dinner together last night barely speaking — a casserole made from some of Garth's gruesome meat, some sort of stewing steak. I couldn't face it — the image of those bloody parcels replayed on a flickering screen deep in my stomach — I thought I might become completely vegetarian. Sheree hadn't been able to finish hers either — Una wasn't much of a cook. I'd filled myself up on muesli.

Tomorrow, of course, tomorrow I would confront Una and ask her what the hell she meant by spinning these stories that were patently untrue. Was she sick, for God's sake? Perhaps that was it. She was truly sick and believed she had been telling the truth. It wasn't as if she could expect to keep this Roy hidden forever.

I found I had picked up the telephone book from the sideboard and was looking for Una's surname in — where? — Wadestown, hadn't she said? And there it was. R for Roy in — Wilton — well, close enough.

The next day I was on my way to meet Roy at a coffee shop near the railway station. The telephone number I'd cheekily dialled was out of date — Una's ex was now living up the coast in Paekakariki — but the new owner of his Wilton home had taken over the phone number and was happy to pass on Roy's details. The gravel voice had quoted no new number when he left his tetchy telephone message, so presumably Una knew these details already. I sat on the trolley bus as it looped around Stewart Dawson's corner, wondering at myself. I could hardly believe I'd been so nosy and so devious as to accept the man's invitation to meet. Sneakily. Or had it been my own idea? I caught the puzzled expression of a woman sitting opposite me and wondered if my face was betraying the judgemental 'look' Una had accused me of wearing. I wasn't being judgemental, I was simply

— well, one had to make moral judgements — what was wrong with that? You couldn't just swing through life thoughtlessly, like a bus, letting people climb on and off at will, indiscriminately. People were supposed to tell the truth surely, for practical reasons: it saved muddle and confusion. It wasn't just an invention of the Presbyterian Church.

I rang the bell before the bus reached the cenotaph and prepared to climb off at the same stop where, as an adolescent, I had leapt from the school tram and transferred to a bus. At fifty-nine I didn't leap. There was nothing wrong with my bones as far as I knew but I seemed incapable of bouncing as I used to. The coffee shop Roy mentioned was past the cenotaph, past the corner of Molesworth Street, several gusts of wind away from the bus stop. I clutched my jacket close so that it wouldn't billow and unsteady me.

Because I'd visited my schooldays so recently in my mind I was nearly put out when the next stretch of the Quay offered unfamiliar buildings, although it also offered new steps leading down to a twenty-first-century coffee shop well protected from the wind. The tables were all unoccupied at that time of day — when the gainfully employed were mostly otherwise engrossed, as Una would be behind her cosmetics counter — so I was free to choose where to plant myself with my latte. The entrance was a wall of glass so I was seated as advantageously as any theatre patron while I watched for him to appear. I wasn't exactly apprehensive, more curious. Una had said so little about her 'deceased' husband that I had no precise idea what he did for a living — something white collar that involved money — or even how he was supposed to have died. Did he know about his death, I wondered. There was always a chance that he was as much of a liar as Una, but I couldn't help looking forward to learning some new angles on the woman who shared my home and mortgage. He would be wanting to learn stuff from me too so I'd have to be careful. Una was my friend, after all, for what it was worth, and you don't betray a friend.

This couldn't be him — not this shuffling old man with a windbreaker and an Alsatian dog that he was having trouble tying to a post. He was lurching inside, limping and mopping his nose on the back of his hand. No. He bought soup and took it in a wobbly grip to the farthest table — perhaps he had seen the look on my face. Was I really as haughty as Una implied? I was so busy thinking about this that I nearly missed the entrance of a second man who had come down the steps quickly and quietly and raised one hand at waist level, signalling doubtfully.

'Yes.' I lifted my own hand, dislodging my cup so that froth spilled into the saucer.

He was a whey-faced businessman who looked as if he shaved his head of all but crisp white stubble. He was wearing the kind of tie I would have expected Una's husband to wear, smart and nondescript at the same time. It wasn't that Una was smart or nondescript but she cared about appearance in the way people do who have little imagination. She did the same sort of thing to her own face every morning so that it was hard to criticise the matt effect but personally I thought her blurred features when she got out of bed first thing looked more friendly. She could certainly have improved on Roy's face. Once he'd been a good-looking man but today he was haggard and sporting a large blackhead beside one eye. The manicured haircut might have been done for my benefit. Una had no doubt told him he had a well-shaped head.

We armed ourselves with coffee and after the first fumbles of conversation I accidentally mentioned Sheree's name. He didn't react. Fourteen-year-old Tyler must have belonged to another part of Una's life. 'She was married before, of course, wasn't she? Una?'

'Oh God, yes. That terrible business.'

'What do you mean?'

'She must talk about it. To *you*. Aren't you an old friend? You said you were an old friend.'

'We were at school, that's all. So what terrible business?'

He was looking embarrassed. 'I can't believe you don't know. Although now I come to think of it she took her time before letting me know who she was.'

'Who she was? Did she say she was somebody different?'

This made him raise his voice in a laugh so that the old man put a hand to his ear, wondering if it was worth eavesdropping. Roy lowered his head and also his voice.

'He was inside when we met — her old man. Lachlan. In Paremoremo. They were already divorced. He came out a few years after but I never met the man and I don't want to. There was a lot of publicity at the time. She kept her own name when she married that bastard and she'd changed Jane's after he went inside so she wasn't really hiding anything. I insisted she take my name when we married, just in case there were people who knew the background. Hardly something . . .'

'So what did he do?'

'You'll have to ask Una. It's not something I talk about.'

'But — Paremoremo?'

'Exactly. It was pretty heavy. The court case sent her mother round the bend — she was already an alkie — and Jane ran off as soon as she was old enough. One of those religious cults got hold of her in America. I always felt a bit guilty that I didn't put my foot down and stop the girl going but we were planning the wedding then. We were happy — mad to think of it now. Didn't last more than a few months, our happy marriage!' He gave a dry snort and drained his coffee cup. 'But we pushed on — as you do.'

'So you don't want her back?'

'What?'

'You said you wanted something back.'

'Oh yes. My share folio. The certificates are no use to her and I've got my own access. But I'm fond of the leather case I kept them in — bought it in Tehran on my first OE. I don't see why she should have that as well as all the money I've handed over. Actually I talked to her about it earlier today, I phoned her at work — I promised not to phone her at home, but she changed her cellphone, didn't she? I've got the number now — so you don't have to pass on any messages. I didn't say we'd spoken.'

There was a dragging silence. The old man had limped past our table and was untying his excited dog. I noticed it was my turn to speak. I cleared my throat but Roy was doing the same, preparing to say more. I waited for it.

'There was something you wanted to ask me?' he said.

'Well — yes.' Then I stopped. 'Do you want another coffee?'

'Not really.'

I turned my cup in its saucer and pulled a warning grimace. 'She told me you were dead!'

'Oh really?' He didn't sound very surprised.

'We even went to the cemetery to visit your grave. Well, I was visiting my husband's grave but she . . .'

'I guess that is taking it a bit far, even for Una.'

'A bit far — yes. Makara cemetery.' Now we could laugh together.

'You didn't exactly need to see me to clear that up. She has trouble with reality sometimes, you must have noticed. But otherwise you get on okay, do you? She doesn't tip glasses of wine into your trousers?'

I felt my jaw drop and raised questioning eyebrows.

'It's just something she likes to do to people who

annoy her. The last party we went to together she yanked me by the belt and emptied a bottle of good chardonnay. Talk about brass monkeys! The woman I was talking to went, "Whoops, I hope he's wearing his Huggies!" That reminds me — I have to be somewhere. My lady friend will be ropeable.' He stood up, reaching for his satchel. 'It was nice meeting you. I don't want Una to be on her own — no, I really don't, no matter what awful things she might say about me. Oh, that's right, I'm dead, aren't I? The grieving widow stuff? I'd keep clear of that if I were you. Let her enjoy it. Did we meet or is it a secret? Up to you of course.'

I sat on after he'd left, bounding up the steps as if he couldn't wait to get away from me. As I watched him go I was wondering if he was one of those people who go to a gym regularly or has a personal trainer. He could probably afford it, by the look of his suit. I took a deep breath and went to order another coffee and a giant blueberry muffin. For some reason I couldn't quite analyse, I was feeling let down, almost as if I'd been expecting him to stay — actually the last thing I wanted — and he'd abandoned me. He'd certainly left rather suddenly. I was glad when the place began to fill up with a huddle of Asian students who chattered in their own tongue. Anyway, I noted — fiercely studying the plastic menu — I had found out something new that I wouldn't have otherwise known. Una clearly hadn't planned to tell me about the jailbird husband, the father of her daughter Jane, and grandfather of Sheree's Tyler. I shook my head over this disbelievingly but it made a

kind of sense. And I didn't have to tell Una any of this
— that I knew her Roy was alive and well, and had a
lady friend. Who had him on the end of a rope and all
she had to do was tug. That was it, I decided — that was
why I felt empty. Una's ex had made me notice how old
I was, how incapable of holding a man's attention as I
would have done only a few years ago, surely. He could
have at least joined me in a second cup of coffee.

Not that I'd have welcomed Roy's attention — God
forbid: he was a boring old businessman with a blackhead
and a self-satisfied smile. Kevin hadn't asked me again to
the champagne bar after I'd turned him down that once.
But no, it wasn't an actual man I was lacking, it was
that aspect of myself that had appealed to one. A facet
of my identity was being stripped from me, along with
the bounce I used to manage alighting from a bus. For
comfort I ran my fingers through my hair — at least I still
had my thick bouncy curls. I knew there were women
who had never bounced, who had never had men making
passes at them, but it was something I'd been used to,
from as far back as schooldays and especially when I
was married. For the first time in my life I was without
a lover. I didn't need one, or want one. I really didn't.
But the fact remained that Una had Garth — funny old
Garth with his faded moustache — and Beryl had her
'friend' Greg and I, Clarice, was the only one who was
completely alone. So alone that I'd sneakily arranged to
meet Una's 'dead' ex in a coffee shop. What a thing to
do. And now I wasn't even sure that I wanted to be in
possession of the knowledge that he'd shared with me.

Una was probably a battered wife at the very least and deserving of sympathy. She'd be good at disguising and concealing bruises that blossomed like rotten fruit, but she'd told me so little.

'We could be good together,' she'd said at the outset, implying just the two of us — and then there was Sheree. Her youth made Sheree nearly as difficult to understand as the Asian students, but lately I'd had the feeling that there was someone there, inside the plump girl with her thin screws of hair and her appetite for sugar and rap songs, someone I might get to know. She had more reason than me to feel alone. I was occupied at the clinic for part of each working week and did a lot of talking with elderly clients and staff, whereas Sheree apparently had no one to talk to apart from other lonely oddballs who roamed Cuba Street, her chosen territory. No wonder she seemed surgically attached to her Walkman. So could Sheree be believed? Could anyone? One of the students at the next table appeared to be playing some kind of game on her cellphone, following her quick fingers with darting brown eyes. At fifty-nine I felt the rules of life had changed so that I didn't know how to play it, any more than I could play a cellphone. Life might feel like a game sometimes but it wasn't about partners now, it was about friends and that made it harder. I didn't know how to play friends, I was too serious. They laughed at me at work for taking things literally. And Una was too elusive. Una was too bloody tricky altogether: she didn't play fair.

# Beryl

Beryl tried to banish the pregnant teenager from her mind, and failed. When she let her library book drop and reached to turn off the lamp the girl's belly swelled to fill a virtual screen in front of her eyes. She heard the flat monotonous sing-song tones complaining that — 'I just want it out'. Beryl had been young too, but not as young as Sheree when she lay in this same room that last time it happened and felt down tremulously for the familiar telltale stickiness between her legs. Donald was at work. When she held her hand above the sheet she knew it would shout brown red, the rough colour of despair. A dark muffled pain in the small of her back but not the pain of childbirth, something less rewarding yet in its own way lingering, unforgettable.

For young Sheree despair was a different colour altogether. She didn't know yet that 'getting rid' could hurt so much, and she would never believe an old woman could know something she did not. Beryl might have been a mother of five and a grandmother by now, knitting for smooth-limbed babies whose skin smelled milky and sweet. Instead what was she? Just old. Did Sheree have no idea what she was giving away? What a waste. At least she hadn't chosen abortion. Beryl felt strongly about abortion. When she had found herself accidentally caught up in an abortion rights march in the seventies, soon after Donald had left her, she had extricated herself, had run away into a shop doorway and shaken it off her like a dog who'd rolled in something oily and nasty. She watched that Friday night trail of marchers, women mostly, swim past her, heads held high, exchanging greetings and grinning happily — some of them — bending their knees and swinging their arms as if it were a sporting event. As she frowned from the shop doorway one woman had frowned back, fiercely, rather like that baboon at the zoo last week. There had been a notice on the cage not to stare for too long because it upset the animals; she didn't see it right away because her eyes were so bad.

She hadn't seen Garth at the zoo recently and wondered if his redundancy had already come into force. Una would know because apparently she and Garth had something going between them — Clarice had told her about it. Her face had twitched curiously as she passed on this news so that Beryl was unsure what she really felt about it, whether the faintly amused pout expressed disgust or pleasure. It could have been either. It had been with Clarice's encouragement that Beryl slipped him the apartment phone number so she must have been a little bit pleased. Beryl had been pushed to visit the zoo last week because again she'd lost Greg and again she had imagined she glimpsed him slipping between the yellow entrance pillars past the advertisement for Zoodoo. She had forgotten to pay but no one stopped her and she remembered only when she found herself outside the baboon enclosure, staring because Greg must have somehow passed through the wire netting, an advantage of being invisible. One of the animals, with a long smoky cape, was raising his eyebrows and baring his canines — was that Greg's doing? — and then he started to grind his teeth and scream, slapping long hands and feet on the ground so that she backed away and ran clumsily in case one of the keepers should appear and remind her that she hadn't purchased a ticket.

She'd felt an idiot, well she *was* an idiot, but she had slowed to a more respectable walk and taken deep slow breaths to bring her blood pressure down. Pulling her shoulder bag higher she had sauntered over to join a group of visitors on the balcony above the giraffe enclosure. Thinking of this she remembered reading somewhere that giraffes gave birth standing up, feet first. For a human that would be a breech birth, not a good thing, she knew that much. Which brought her back to Sheree and her gravid belly. Beryl wouldn't have minded standing up so long as she'd delivered a baby and not a giraffe — or would she? What did she know about giving birth really? Nothing. She sat up in bed and reached for the light switch.

Greg was sitting in his duffel coat at the foot of her bed, smiling expectantly.

'Oh, there you are,' she said. 'So what business did you have with the baboons? That was you making them angry, wasn't it?'

'It was you, you silly woman. Didn't you read the notice? Too much eye contact.'

'I suppose you think I'm a silly old woman wanting Sheree's baby. But she doesn't want it. She wants to give it away. She could give it to me!'

'She'll have made other arrangements, you know that.'

Beryl fished with her toes under the bed, trawling for her slippers. She was trying to remember whether there was any tonic left in the fridge. 'I don't know anything.'

'And you're far too old.'

'Am I? Sometimes I don't feel old enough, I'm still learning how to be alive.'

'You're old enough to buy gin.'

'Well, that's true. Will you come with me while I get it? I miss you when you stay away for such a long chunk of time. It isn't just my eyes, is it?' Outside the bedroom window the musical chorus of blackbird and thrush was obliterated by a series of eerie howls and soaring calls from the zoo home of the gibbons. Beryl's night was nearly over and she couldn't remember if she'd had any shut-eye at all, but when you're sixty-four sleep doesn't matter the same. It used to be the most important thing. Her mother had told her there was something wrong with her, all the sleep she needed, but that was when she was young, when they'd find her snoozing on the bedroom floor as if she didn't know where the bed was. Why had she done that — sagged into slumber? Was it wrong? Of course it was wrong — it was weakness. Worse than wrong.

Narcolepsy didn't exist when Beryl started babysitting at sixteen and there was no point in acknowledging it now, owning up to weakness. Giving it the name she came across in *Time* magazine in the seventies wouldn't change what had happened. The wee girl had run out to meet the family car when it turned into the drive and where was the babysitter? There was no excuse for the 'tragic accident' Beryl woke up to that ghastly day, pretending she had never been asleep. And the face of the child's mother! Nightmare stuff. Beryl woke up to it over and again, even some mornings in 2002, sloshing in her head like a greasy toxin. Narcolepsy was a syndrome, not a sin, but for Beryl it weighed the same so she kept it a secret, from herself as well the others. Maybe God had decided she was guilty and taken her babies away to protect them, so it wouldn't happen again. But she'd be on guard in the future, armed to the teeth, the best mother in the history of the world; God wasn't listening. Beryl had thought about this often, of course, but you can learn not to think when it matters enough.

*I* don't get it.' Sheree was puzzled. 'Why? I mean he's awful, that Garth. And she's past it, she must be.'

We were walking together on Riddiford Street.

'Why must she be? You don't have any idea, do you?'

'Yes I do. I'm used to old people.'

'Why's that?'

'I don't have to tell you my life.'

'No, you don't,' I agreed. 'But I am interested.'

'Why? You can't possibly be interested. Nosy, more like.'

'You don't seem to have anyone apart from Una. There must be a mother somewhere in your life.'

'If you say so.'

'Someone found you under a gooseberry bush, is that what you're saying?'

Sheree snorted. 'All right, if you must know Mum got run over by a taxi when I was a little kid. She was drunk, wasn't she. That's when I went to my grandma and then she got too old and sick and I stayed with her sister, my Aunty Lyn. That's what I mean — I know all about mad old people.'

'We're not old — I don't suppose your grandma was old either — and we're certainly not mad.'

'You want a bet?'

We were walking to the supermarket because Una had taken her car and was spending the weekend with Garth at his flat that was on a main road two streets away from the zoo. She had explained that she had to do this since I'd been so unwelcoming and also because the ribbed glass doors to her bedroom were not soundproofed, which could be embarrassing. They might want to make noises. Perhaps I ought not to have repeated this last bit of information but I did need to share it with somebody and the young were known to be less narrow-minded.

Sheree walked with her left hand on her back as if her tummy needed support and, glancing at her sideways, I wondered if it had been a good idea to ask for her company. It was quite a step to the supermarket.

'Are you okay?'

''Course.'

'You can listen to your music if you want.'

'I know I can. Who's going to stop me?' She pressed her lips together and wriggled them comically under her nose. 'Isn't this where your Beryl hangs out? This street?'

'No — she's right up the end, near the zoo. And she's not mine.'

'Isn't she your friend?'

'Oh well . . .'

'My friends are all in Sydney. That's why I don't have anyone to hang out with here. I'll go back when I've dropped the tadpole.'

'Is that why you came over? To drop — to have the baby? What was wrong with Sydney? I thought you said you had friends.'

'Nothing wrong.' She shook her head, scowling. 'I got scared. They aren't that kind of friends — you wouldn't understand.'

'And your aunty?'

'Hah! She's no use. She hates my guts anyway. Una doesn't ask questions.'

'Or answer them.'

'What?'

We had drawn level with the mall entrance and I put out a steering hand. I was remembering another occasion when Sheree had followed us to this supermarket and made a ridiculous scene, screaming as if she were a naughty child who couldn't get her own way. She'd improved since then anyway. Without really trying we must have been having a good effect on the girl.

# Beryl

In a kitchen down the road Beryl talked to Greg Preston about the baby, Sheree's baby, just as she had talked to him about those other babies who turned back before their journey was over and never arrived to fill her impatient arms. She talked to him today and he was sympathetic: she knew he would be because he had understood so well on other occasions. He might answer back and tease her, but in important things he understood. The accident when she was babysitting was different — she couldn't put that in words even for Greg, she wasn't sure why that was. Hearing those words spill out of her mouth . . . No. Some sort of celestial jury might be listening, ready to judge her. But she could safely share Sheree's baby with Greg. When he was around . . .

Sometimes these days while she was talking to Greg she was aware that he faded — he didn't quite leave but was no longer fully visible until she gave him her complete attention and concentrated hard, bringing him back into the living room, the bedroom. She remembered telling him — not entirely seriously — that the other week she had imagined she saw him on television and he was incredibly aged, thinner and with fluffy white hair, pretending to be someone quite other than himself, an older English gentleman. She had laughed because it was so idiotic but so perfect that Greg couldn't, wouldn't age, as she had to. Perhaps it had been a mistake to joke about it and let even a chink of the actor role meet the light of day. But surely Greg knew he was not an actor playing a part — she had never looked up something so silly as those details in the *Listener* programme pages — but a character conceived and born with distinctive television DNA as surely as babies are conceived and born of other human beings. He couldn't turn back as the babies in her own womb had done.

'Breastfeeding remains the best option,' Greg said rather surprisingly.

'Where did you get that from? Some magazine?' She must throw out that awful withered pile on the wash-house shelf. 'Anyway they have ever such cute bottles in the supermarket, not too big and not too small. And funny-shaped dummies that fit the roof of the mouth perfectly. I don't think they cost much.'

'Isn't it time you filled up that silly wheelie bag again? The fridge is looking pretty empty and the tomatoes are mush.'

'You're absolutely right. I have to feed myself as well, don't I? Don't want to turn into an Old Mother

Hubbard.' She put out a hand and pulled the shabby bag on wheels from behind the door. 'Promise me you'll still be here when I get back.'

'Promise you won't buy a dummy,' Greg said, making her laugh.

Clarice and Sheree were two streets away by the time she reached the mall. She left the supermarket entrance feeling unusually happy with fresh fruit and cauliflower and a shrink-wrapped, bright yellow rubber pacifier.

*T*he annual meeting of the building's body corporate was to be held in Marge's living room. We'd argued about whether we should both attend.

'They don't want me sticking my oar in,' Una pleaded, her upper lip lumpy with distaste. 'You know how Kevin feels about me — he snubbed me, remember, twice. Marge doesn't like me, and the bloody dog can't stand the way I smell.'

'The dog. Exactly. I don't fancy that soppy little creature panting all over me.'

'She wants one of us to go. And we do need to know what's going on with the windows.' Clumsy scaffolding had recently appeared outside the living room, shading some of our view to the east. 'You know you've got your eye on Kevin.'

'I haven't! He's not interested in me.'

'Or there's that old chap in the bedsit. Perhaps you'd prefer him.'

'Now you're being unpleasant.'

'No more than he is.' The ancient occupant of the ground-floor bedsit was disabled and irritable. He played opera far too loudly, leaving his door ajar, and rejected any kindly meant advance. We'd seen the visiting hospital nurse and the woman from Meals on Wheels leaving his apartment looking worn and despondent.

'He won't go, will he? Marge says he keeps to himself,' I reminded her.

'Well, there you are — it won't matter if I don't go either. I'm going to watch *Mercy Peak* with Sheree. But you go. You might get useful. Take a notebook with you.'

Marge's living room was much as she described it. Toby jugs decorated a glossy mahogany sideboard and the Queen, pictured during her first visit to New Zealand, raised an imperial chin above cruelly compressed breasts so that her youthful, piercing tones were nearly visible shooting across the lacy tablecloth. Kevin, who was acting secretary of the body corporate, rested his laptop apologetically upon this surface and grimaced at me faintly, almost as if he sensed an ally. We were closer in age than Marge, who must have been nearing seventy and wore a tulip-shaped skirt with a high-necked blouse, while I was wearing my jeans. There were only a few residents present so there was no excuse for formality and it was perfectly appropriate that Marge had produced pikelets to go with the tea. She leaned down to offer India a portion of one of these, complete with jam, while Kevin read from a list on his laptop, explaining that his printer had let him down at the last minute or we would have had hard copies of the report. There was a moment when I felt irresistibly tempted to laugh, although there was really nothing funny about the increase in rates or the cost of painting the east side of the building. I controlled myself. What did I have to feel superior about?

Our apartment was only one floor down so when it was time to leave I took the stairs. I was wondering how long Marge had occupied her odd rooms and promising myself our kitchen would never look as hectic as hers. Behind me I heard the door flop shut and was suddenly aware of Kevin, juggling laptop and briefcase, hanging back so as not to push past me rudely on the narrow steps.

He breathed at my left ear. 'Come in for a drink?'

'Shall I?'

'Yes please.'

Together we passed the door that led to my floor. Una and Sheree would be watching television. I felt a secret pleased smile playing with my lips. Just a drink, I told Una silently. And yet I did feel a whole lot better. I was still recognisably myself after all. It was something resembling the feeling that possessed you while you waited to uplift luggage from the claim area after a trip overseas. I was back on familiar territory and soon I would be unpacking familiar items that belonged to me alone and would make my life comfortable, if not exciting. Hang on, slow down, I told myself. I was fifty-nine years old and didn't need another sexual relationship, even supposing it were on offer.

Kevin's apartment was smaller than Una's and mine but somehow more confident. How had he managed this without a woman's touch? Money, perhaps. The small leather sofa was crushed with age and the occasional table ringed with the ghosts of hot coffee cups. A large dark wooden desk with pigeon holes had a built-in leather flap that didn't quite conceal two bottles and a shelf of sparkling glasses. The far side of this desk carried an imposing printer — the one that presumably didn't work. Kevin lowered his laptop onto an old-fashioned blotter beside this printer and slotted his briefcase into the space between desk and sofa, before he reached for a bottle.

'Sorry. This is all I've got. Gin or Scotch?'

I wouldn't have been surprised to see him open another leather flap in the desk to reveal a fridge but for this he had to walk some distance and reach behind a tall tiled kitchen bar, returning with bottles of tonic and soda clamped between spread fingers. I'd dumped my bottom casually into a less than comfortable small blue armchair, leaving the sofa for him. Instead he chose to sit on the black office chair in front of the desk and swivelled it closer. 'Thanks.' I looked sideways, seeking the bathroom which I guessed would be directly below ours. This was the man I'd visualised sitting on the loo browsing a seedy magazine while water dripped on him from the ceiling above. I choked slightly on my gin and tonic and felt my face going pink.

'Too strong?'

'No, it's great.'

'I usually need a drink after one of those meetings. I'm not sure why: nothing very drastic ever happens. Marge used to be in charge before I moved in, but she was keen for me to take over. Your turn next for the committee — how about it?'

'I'd rather not. You haven't asked me here about that?'

'Of course I haven't. I suppose I thought you might like to see this flat now that you've seen Marge's.'

'Do you see much of your neighbour? I'm glad we didn't overflow into his bathroom.'

'Crabby Colin? You were lucky actually — his bathroom backs onto mine. He'd have been worse than me.'

'I thought you were quite reasonable, considering. It could have been a disaster. It's a nice apartment this one, nicer than ours. So how long have you been here?'

'Not long. I transferred from Auckland when I found myself on my own a couple of years back. I'm still getting used to Wellington but the job's more interesting. I read somewhere that moving house is as stressful as a death but I don't believe it.'

'Your wife died,' I said, less a question than a bleak sense of here we go again.

'She didn't actually. She got homesick and decided she had to go back to London. Her father's there and our son as well. I visit her twice a year — it's not too difficult with the job I'm in. And that's it.'

'Goodness. That's different. Long-distance marriage. But you're lucky if you can travel. So what is it you do?'

'Customs. We came out here for the job because — well, it's my country and I love it and I can't stomach England. It just gets worse. And Blair gets a lot worse. Besides I enjoy my work. I feel I'm doing something worthwhile, specially since September 11. We're employing a lot of new trainees. I could never get anything like this in England. In England I'd be a pensioner next year and I'd much rather be a working man. She gets her pension this year too and she likes the idea of travelling free on the tube. You work, don't you?'

'Just part time now. An audiology clinic. It's a rising market; but I'm not qualified — or not in audiology. I used to work for a law firm and then the Post Office when it existed — I'm afraid I'm a bit dull.'

'Don't put yourself down. I used to do that until my wife taught me not to.' His face crumpled suddenly into a warm smile that startled me because it was so attractive and so unexpected. The angles of his chin and cheek altered subtly and laugh lines appeared, leading into a pale, hazel depth of eye contact.

'Oh.' I stared, then recovered, putting out one hand to hold tightly to an arm of the blue chair. 'Did you? You must miss her awfully.'

'I think I'm a bit of a workaholic. That probably helps. And the sex — well, it's not like when you're twenty something, is it?'

'Isn't it? No, no, of course it isn't.'

'So the pregnant young person — who does she

belong to? Is she yours? A daughter?'

I felt flattered for a moment until I realised that was probably his intention. But why shouldn't it be possible? Lots of women gave birth these days in their forties and some even, with help, in their fifties. I thought of my clever Sophie, tall, slim and beautiful, and despised myself for imagining even for one moment that I could also be mother to someone like Sheree. I shook my head rather violently. 'No, not me. She's Una's responsibility.' The same word Una used to describe the relationship; it saved explanation. 'My two are both living overseas. Stuart's in Australia and Sophie's in Berlin. Sometimes it feels as if half the people I know are somewhere else.' Now he's going to ask about my husband, I thought, and sighed because I used to get a kick out of telling people about myself, but suddenly it felt like a chore I'd rather get out of.

'You're divorced, aren't you? Marge said. Or are you the widow?'

'I'm both. Widowed, and then I married again.'

'It didn't work out? That sounds about normal to me. Fifty per cent of marriages fall apart — I read that somewhere. I guess I'm lucky.'

'Not exactly lucky, living on two sides of the world!'

'You hear quite often about couples who choose to live apart — marriage is something else now, isn't it? But you're right, it's too bloody far away.' He pulled a face that was at once pitiable and engaging.

I drained the last of my gin. I didn't know whether to

be pleased or sorry that his wife was overseas. I'd been shocked at the way my insides moved and fell into a puddle of tiny broken pieces when I saw that wry smile again. Damn. I stared into my empty glass but couldn't see any guidance there.

'Have another?'

I jerked and very nearly dropped the glass on the carpet. 'Whoops. No, I don't think I should really.'

'Come on, why not? Do you have to be somewhere?' He was already tipping the Bombay Sapphire into my glass and I watched, mesmerised. The blue of the bottle was enchanting.

So what did he want of me? He was happily married, and sex wasn't really a problem for him. What did that leave? Friendship? Neighbourliness? It was true I'd been vaguely interested when we learned there was a personable single man living below us, and yes I'd been pleased when he asked me to try out the champagne bar with him and disappointed that I had to turn him down. But personable bore no relation to the adjective I was seeking to describe him now. How had he done this? Something in the gin? But I knew it was no more than the way his face became animated when he was relaxed, almost as if he enjoyed my company, as if — yes — as if he found me attractive. Or perhaps amiable. Nothing dangerous about amiable.

'Tell me more about your wife. Is that her photograph on the piano? Oh, do you play?' I heard myself starting to babble, making clumsy conversation. 'And what *is* this?' I had stood up and reached out to handle a curious sculpture so surprisingly heavy I nearly dropped it.

Kevin shot out a hand and for a moment we were both holding the sculpture and our thumbs touched. 'It's some sort of bird. I'm not really sure.' He was looking apologetic now — and something else. His thumb moved against mine. There was no doubt about it: I hadn't imagined the innuendo which deepened in his expression until it became an invitation. This was awful. Amazing and awful. More than awful was knowing I would go along with him, at least as far as the bedroom — it was behind ribbed glass doors, like Una's — thinking already how tight my jeans were and wondering how on earth would I gracefully get myself out of them.

It must have been at least an hour later when I lay on the bed with him gazing at a spider on the ceiling without blinking. 'Wow.'

'Wow? Is that good?'

'I came.'

'That's what it's about. Don't you always?'

'No, not always. Not for years — in fact I can't remember coming with Lester. Ever. That's my last husband.' It's funny how sex can loosen your tongue.

'Good God. So why now?'

'I don't know. Lester was a bit lazy — he'd do it with his hands behind his back if he could. But that's not it really. I suppose — it felt as if you meant it.'

'Meant it?'

I rolled on one elbow, keeping the sheet firmly under my chin. My breasts were fifty-nine years old. 'Yes.'

He had a worried look on his face. 'You thought I might be going to fall in love with you — is that it?'

I was embarrassed. 'No, no. Of course not. Or not — not *love* exactly.'

'Well, I won't. Clarice, I'm sorry — I can't do this to you. It was a fuck. A gorgeous fuck. And it's a deadly secret if you ever meet my wife, which you will. She comes over when she can. And that means keeping your lips sealed. Okay? You mustn't tell — what's-her-name — Una. Promise me.'

'But I can't! I can't not tell Una.'

'Don't you ever have secrets from each other?'

'No!' I lied. 'Well — sometimes maybe.' I'd never been tempted to lay bare my sexual feelings to Una — that was for husbands — and as for love, I couldn't believe I'd allowed the word into the conversation instead of banishing it immediately. I was angry that he'd manipulated this exposure from me, a more careless kind of undressing than peeling off my tight jeans. I looked for a diverting gambit but was distracted by a curtain of tears blinding me and coursing down my cheeks to fall on the back of my hand.

'You're crying.' It was his turn to be embarrassed.

I sobbed.

He frowned. 'Why do you have to tell anyone? I don't get it.'

'I'm not crying at that.'

'Oh.' He bowed his head apologetically.

'But I have to talk to someone about it, if I can't even talk to you.'

'You can talk to me. Sometimes. We might even do it again. But discreetly. All right? Are you all right?' He brushed my hair back, looking for my face. 'You're a lovely lady, you know. Lovely.'

When I let myself into the apartment it wasn't late — or not very late. Kevin and I had had a drink together: that was allowed. I hadn't told Una how he'd asked me to the champagne bar a few weeks ago because I had needed to protect her feelings, but she was okay now and besides, she had Garth, didn't she? Horrible Garth. No, that wasn't fair — the man wasn't horrible, he just wasn't very nice. It wasn't the bulging white forehead so much as the metallic ring of his voice. And whatever did they talk about? Animals? Kevin had been sceptical about Garth's job at the zoo, claiming they were looking for people with university qualifications these days or close enough and that he sounded too old anyway to have landed the job only a few years before as he claimed. I pointed out that this was probably why they sacked him but Kevin protested that there had to be a reason beyond the date on his birth certificate. Anyway what did it matter so long as Una was happy.

She raised her face, tapping the television remote control so that the picture dissolved. 'You took a long time?'

It was a question and I had to answer it. I'd spent some minutes attempting to erase all evidence of what had been going on in the bedroom directly below Una's, but I was all too aware that my lips were denuded of lipstick — I hadn't bothered to take my handbag just to go upstairs to Marge's place. I'd asked Kevin if his wife had left any lipstick behind but there was nothing useful of hers except a bottle of Clear Eyes, which I'd borrowed gratefully. Did Kevin make his wife cry too? Well, of course he did: he let her to go to England all on her own. I'd found an old packet of Throaties in the bathroom cupboard and licked one, smearing the sticky lozenge on my lips until there was some pinkness deposited there. When I'd looked in the mirror behind the door I thought I looked fairly normal. Una wouldn't notice.

'What's wrong with your face? What have you been up to? You didn't!'

'No, I didn't,' I lied, blushing. I walked away from her and pretended to be busy at the bench. 'We did have a drink. More than one in fact. I need to go to the loo.' When I came out of the bathroom, my face repaired, Una was still watching expectantly, waiting for details.

'So what's the story with the windows?'

'What?'

'The scaffolding? Do we have to pay extra for the paint job?'

'Oh — yes. Just a bit. It's all right, I can afford it if you can't.'

'He tried it on, didn't he? Where did you have a drink? His place?'

'Okay, I let him kiss me. That's all. He's married you know — his wife's in England. He loves her.'

'Oh. He seems to have told you quite a lot about himself.'

'Why shouldn't he? He's nice. He's a really nice man.'

'Ooh.' Una pulled a face. 'I knew you fancied him.'

Sheree hadn't been listening to any of this. Head encased in earphones as usual, she was moving her hips rhythmically in front of the windows at the far side of the living room where the light was switched off to save on power and the moon glinted between shafts of scaffolding. She waved at me and I smiled. I'd lied and it hardly hurt at all.

When Una was suffering one of her moods it changed the colour of her face so that the pale skin looked bruised and her plucked, pencilled eyebrows settled into a taut, straighter line. She leaned on propped elbows, pressing fingers into the sides of her brow as if trying to crush something inside her head.

I asked her, 'Have you taken something?'

'What for?'

'You don't look very well.'

'Thank you very much!' Una spat.

'I'm just trying to help.'

'You can't help. No one can help, because there's nothing bloody wrong. Did I say there was anything wrong?'

'No.'

'So piss off.'

Una had returned after spending Saturday night with Garth so it seemed evident that her mood was related to this. I rummaged in my brain for a way of broaching the subject without making matters worse.

'It isn't Garth,' Una denied before I could say anything. 'He's perfectly fine. We rolled around together on his rug, as we do. He's only got a single bed. It's nothing to do with Garth. It's me. I'm a fucking disaster.'

'I can't see how.'

'Well, you wouldn't. You're so bloody good at everything, how could you possibly know what it's like to be me!'

I shivered because this gust blew threateningly close to my own thoughts. 'Well, that's nonsense. What am I so good at?'

'You want a list? That's typical.'

'I don't want a list. I just — oh, forget it.'

It shouldn't matter whether I got on well with Una — we were only 'tenants in common'; it wasn't as if we were a couple. But I'd had such hopes for this new beginning in a city apartment. Friendship must surely be easier than marriage. But curiously it felt harder, more dangerous, perhaps because the rules were less obvious and I'd had less practice at living so closely with a woman friend. Of course Una was difficult. And we didn't really talk to each other as women are meant to do, sharing secrets and confessions, swapping feelings as easily as recipes and earrings. I'd blamed Una for this but maybe I was as much to blame.

Propped on a kitchen stool pretending to read the weekend paper, I wished I could talk carelessly about my adventure with Kevin and somehow take the edge off it. It was chafing me uncomfortably. But if I'd been free to talk, it might well have made my relationship with Una worse. I couldn't forget that it was she who first attempted closeness with Kevin and how shaken she was when it failed. I looked at Una's bowed head and her tortured frown and felt lonely.

'I'm going to the dairy for some chocolate. Do you want anything?' I asked first Una and then Sheree, who was ironing a wide purple shirt on the floor.

'If you scorch my carpet I'll kill you,' Una lifted her head to say.

'Our carpet,' I corrected, catching her irritable mood. 'So, do you? Want anything?'

'No thanks. Well, maybe a winning Lotto ticket.'

I grabbed my handbag and was nearly down the stairs before I changed my mind about chocolate and folded up on one of the steps, thinking. I cupped my chin in my hands and listened to the silence of the building. To my left the door to Kevin's floor was only inches away and if I sat for long enough he might appear, glance up and notice me. Of course I could go and knock on his door, but I wouldn't. That would be pathetic. He could have phoned.

Sitting there, I was reminded of an occasion when I waited at a city council tram stop for a schoolfriend: we'd planned to spend an afternoon at the fairground of the Winter Show. The friend hadn't turned up but I sat on, too shamed to go home and tell Mother that I was unloved and abandoned. I'd sat in the shelter all afternoon while tram after tram deposited passengers who dispersed busily to go about their lives while I just slumped there, reading the graffiti until it was time for me to go home. This kind of abandonment and disappointment was too embarrassing: I never confessed to it. I must have nodded my head when asked if I'd had a good time. Now there was no graffiti to distract me as I sat on the unyielding green-carpeted stair, looking at the lumpy cream wall.

A noise that wasn't quite a creak announced the swing doors admitting someone from on the street. Upgraded security had been one of the subjects discussed at the meeting in Marge's English lounge but so far everyone was content with the current system, which meant that until seven in the evening anyone was free to enter the building without a key. I lurched to my feet, feeling a bit silly sitting there and nearly hopeful that it might be someone I knew. It was: Beryl! I laughed with surprise to see her about to mount the steps, a slightly balding section of scalp visible in a ray of light from the slitted window.

'Hello! For goodness' sake — Beryl! I thought you'd forgotten the address. I was just on my way out, but I'm not going anywhere, just the dairy. I told Una I'd get her a Lotto ticket. Will you walk with me, and we can get some muffins? I don't think Sheree's left any biscuits in the tin.'

Some ball game was in progress inside the Basin Reserve and cars were thronging, swooping across lanes, impatient on their way to find parking spaces. We walked past the imposing entrance to Government House and kept on walking, talking above the cries and whoops from the sporting ground. 'It's a bit like school, eh? I hated sports day, not like Una.'

'Did you really? I thought I was unusual when I hid in the bushes with a book. So what did Una do?'

'Everything. Tennis mostly. We didn't really know each other at school.' And don't know each other now. At the same moment I thought, I can tell Beryl about Kevin. The idea comforted me even while I was deciding to put it off until another time. 'How about your Greg? Will he be watching the game on the box?'

Beryl gave a little laugh. 'Sport on the box — I can't stand sport on television. I just have to get away.'

'Well, I'm glad you did. Una's in one of her moods and Sheree's not much better. You'll be good for them.'

'It can't be too far off now.'

I looked puzzled.

'The baby.'

'Oh, the baby. I think it's a couple of months. We don't talk about it a lot. Una's not too happy about being a great-grandmother. Crazy to think of, really. I told you the father was only fourteen, didn't I?"

'But you must have done some shopping. There's so much you have to buy for a little one.'

'I suppose you've been there. How many grand-children in your life?'

'Me? None. We couldn't manage a family, Don and I.'

'Oh God, I'm sorry. How could I forget? You did tell me. I really am a clod sometimes. I can't imagine how you must feel. I've got no siblings — I know what that's like. Is there no one . . . ? What about Greg's family?'

'No. Just the two of us.' She ducked her head, flushing

with embarrassment. 'I mean . . .'

'I had a favourite aunty who spoiled me when I was little. I've got a koala bear for the new arrival but I hid it because Una laughed at me. You know Sheree's arranged to have the baby adopted?'

'You mean she just hands it over? I don't know how she can do that! None of my business, of course. She'll have had adoption counselling, I suppose.'

I shrugged as we walked into the dairy and the two warning notes sounded. 'Will she? I don't know anything about that.'

'Oh yes. I think it's compulsory. I did a bit of research once when Don and I were thinking about — well, just me really, he wasn't so sure. Of course everything's changed since then . . .'

We were crossing the road to the apartment before Sheree's name came up again. Beryl wanted to know if she had anyone to go to antenatal classes with her and I realised I knew next to nothing about the girl. For all I knew Sheree might have had the photo of a scan and multiple pamphlets about childbirth hidden under her bed. 'She's booked in at Wellington Public. I don't know what happens after that. Una's got it all sorted but she's a bit touchy about the subject — you might as well be warned.'

Kevin's name signalled to me from the letterboxes in the foyer as we headed for the lift. I felt again the weight of the lead sculpture — a bird, he had said — resting in my hand and then his cool fingers touching mine. Something like a bird had spread wings inside me that day and the memory ached to fly again. Bugger.

# Beryl

Beryl hung out the washing while she talked to Greg, who was pacing on the swollen shoulder of the garden in his duffel coat and peaked cap. She pouched the faded, striped sheets before pegging them so that they would catch the wind, and hung her underwear discreetly — involving a delicate twist so that her knickers radiated no hint of intimacy should the neighbours be looking. But all the time she was keeping her eye on Greg so that he didn't slide off her range of vision while she told him about her visit to Clarice's apartment.

'I don't believe she's happy about it really — the adoption idea. I'm not even sure Una's happy — Clarice thinks she might not like the idea of being a great-grandmother. I read somewhere that the emphasis is on responsibility these days, rather than rights. The girl might not want to exercise her right to contact with the child once it's born, but she still has a responsibility to own up to its DNA.'

'You don't know what you're talking about,' Greg laughed at her. 'What do you know about DNA and responsibility? You just want to hold her and give her a bath and pretend you're not sixty-four years old.'

'That's not true. I'm fine with being sixty-four. I could give her a bath without dropping her — or him. What makes you think she's a girl?'

'She?' Now Greg was laughing at her, that deep nasal gurgle dancing between the flapping tea-towels she had just finished pegging on the line.

'All right, I'm a silly old lady.' She turned her back on him haughtily, then whipped around, checking that she hadn't frightened him away. He was still there, still smiling, but quite kindly now. 'I knew you'd understand. You know how much it matters to me. I could help with a baby — I know I could. I'd really appreciate anything you can think of to make it happen.'

She hoisted the empty plastic basket against her chest and as she did so caught sight of a dark jacket moving beside the house to the back gate. How had he moved so fast? And why was he running away again? No, he hadn't gone. For when she hung the basket inside the door he was behind her. She was pleased, but confused, and pushed her glasses up to rub her eyes briskly.

*Sheree was staring in her bedroom mirror and Tyler was standing behind her staring over her shoulder. Damp prickles of hair clutched his bony scalp and she could feel the gun pressing against her hip. He thought it turned her on, but it didn't, it made her feel weak and sick like she might be going to throw up. She told him this but he laughed.*

*'Nah. You're pregnant that's what. I'm gonna die and you're going to have my kid. I tell you, if my kid does anything like I've done I'll kill him. If I'm alive.'*

*'You're not going to die. Why are you going to die?'*

*'They'll get me. They always get you. Four of my friends got done. There's nowhere far enough.'*

*In the mirror Sheree moved sideways to hide his face and his quivering lip. She punched the mirror and reached behind her for the Walkman.*

In the living room Una had the television on full bore but she didn't seem to be watching it, there was a distracted expression on her face. She jumped when Sheree pushed past her. 'Oh. You going out?'

'Might as well. You are.'

'What d'you mean?'

'You've got your coat on.'

'I've been out.' Una shrugged the black raincoat off her shoulders and hung it carelessly on the coat stand. 'I can't find Clarice.'

'What do you want her for?'

'Nothing. I just thought I'd look for her. It's Sunday.'

'She'll be in church then, eh.' This was a joke and gave them an excuse to laugh together.

Clarice was not in church. When Una was searching the bathroom cupboard for paracetamol Clarice was beneath her feet, blotting herself dry on Kevin's canary-yellow towel.

My mouth felt swollen, Botoxed with pleasure when I stroked lipgloss across the phantom of his fierce kisses. I'd remembered my handbag this time and didn't have to resort to sticky cough sweets. In the living room he was pouring aromatic coffee from a steel carafe into wide yellow cups with a daisy on the side.

'I can't send you home without a coffee, can I?'

'You want to get rid of me?'

'No! That's not what I'm saying.' He glanced at the wall clock. 'It's been a couple of hours. I didn't mean to go to sleep. I've got some papers I need to . . . I'm on a late shift.'

'It's all right, I should be getting back. After this.' I picked up the cup and held its warmth close to my chin, breathing in the comforting smell.

Kevin reached for my other hand and stroked it.

'You're not cold? Shall I put on the heater? It's getting to be that time of year.'

'No, no I'm fine. This is lovely.'

He smiled and moved in closer. 'It was lovely, wasn't it? I'm lucky to have you so close at hand. I knew I could trust you to be discreet. Only someone as moral as you could turn me down because it might upset her friend. Don't you know the saying all's fair in love and war?' He laughed at me and his eyes crinkled in the way that made my stomach jump.

I looked down into my coffee. 'There are different rules for war these days — you're supposed to fight fair. Soldiers are peacemakers, right?'

'So you think the rules for love are changing too? Don't seem to be any hard and fast rules so far as I can make out.'

'But you make rules yourself! You think it's okay to fuck me because your wife's in England — so long as I keep my mouth shut.'

'Nothing new about that rule. And I'm glad you didn't want to upset Una. I'm all for friendship — that's what we are, isn't it? Friends?'

'Is that what we are?'

'Well — with extras of course.'

'You could try Vivian Street instead, if you want young.'

'Oops. You're mad at me. Why? I don't need young.'

'I'm sorry. I'm not mad at you. I just thought — prostitution's legal now. Of course it's a bit of a walk to Vivian Street and I'm right here.'

'Clarice! I don't want just sex. If you're not happy we won't do it at all.'

I gulped at my coffee so carelessly it slopped into the saucer and made me cough. 'Don't say that. I am happy. That's the trouble, I suppose. I'm just not used to this. I don't have affairs, not since I grew up and got married. I've always been married.'

'You haven't always been happy.'

'Mmm — most of the time. And then I was in shock after David died.'

'What about sex? You said . . .'

'Forget what I said. That wasn't fair of me to say that. Lester was a good man although he wasn't always faithful. And he could piss me off. Yes.' I paused. 'I don't know why we stayed together as long as we did.'

'People get scared of change. I was scared when Dale went.'

'You're not scared now?'

'Why would I be? I've got everything I need — and Dale too. She's just not here.'

'You're still going to die.'

'Oh yeah, there's that. Goodness, you are a cheerful person when you get out of bed.'

'Sorry. I'm not really like this. I'd better go. I said I'd cook tonight.'

By the time I let myself into the apartment a cosy fried-onion aroma was already scenting the kitchen. I apologised to Una and explained I was visiting a friend.

'What friend? Not Beryl.'

'No.' I was puzzled. Why should I have been at Beryl's, I had plenty of other friends. Or had I? It seemed to have become a habit for my contemporaries to move outside the city as they got older, or up the coast, a train journey or at least a bus trip away, leaving their crooked steps and twisted paths behind to wrestle with the Wellington wind. 'I haven't been inside Beryl's place — she hasn't asked me. What's in the oven then?'

'A casserole. Nearly the last of Garth's meat.'

'Oh God.'

'Never mind God. I cut it up without any help from him, in proper bite-sized pieces this time. Sheree's gone walkabout. I gave her some money so we don't have to wait for her. Shouldn't be too long — I just put the spuds in.' She tugged at the fridge door. 'I need a G and T. How about you? Or have you started without me?'

Una almost sounded like a jealous spouse, who had been waiting at home for me, slaving in the kitchen. 'We had coffee, that's all.' I might as well be as truthful as possible.

'She's a nutter. A raving nutter,' Una said, handling her gin clumsily, as if it might be her third drink or even more.

'Sheree?'

'No, that Beryl.'

'I don't know what you're talking about. Why is Beryl a nutter?'

'Goodness knows why, but she is. She talks to herself. I went round there looking for you and . . .'

'Are you sure you got the right house?'

'Of course I got the right house — I can read street numbers. She was in the garden talking to herself. It was embarrassing. I didn't stay — I came right on home.'

I gave a little laugh. 'People do talk to themselves sometimes. When they're on their own. I've done it myself. Just the other day I was walking along the road and I didn't know there was someone behind me. Felt a real fool.'

'But you're not mad. I think Beryl is. Some of the things she said . . .'

'Like what?'

'I can't remember exactly. It was like she really believed someone was answering her. I don't think you should get too close to her.'

'Don't be silly. Why not? Perhaps someone else was there and you just couldn't see them.'

'No.' Una shook her head. 'She's a case. A nutcase. Why are you laughing at me? I suppose you think I'm the nutter. Just because I saw a therapist . . . it takes courage to see someone professional. You wouldn't understand something like that.'

Oh God, I told myself. She's in a mood. I'm going to have to eat a whole plateful of her bloody casserole and humour her or keep my mouth shut. But then I heard myself saying, 'You're right, it must take guts. So perhaps Beryl needs a therapist. You could be sympathetic instead of judging her. And you say *I'm* judgemental!'

'When? I've never said any such thing.'

'But you have!' Suddenly I'd had enough of skirting around the words I really wanted to say. 'I don't know.

*159*

Is there something wrong with your memory or are you just a liar? We know you tell lies.'

'I beg your pardon?'

'Going to the cemetery to visit your dear departed husband! He's not departed and he's not dear either. I had lunch with him last week.' I noticed belatedly this wasn't quite true.

Una was staring. 'You what? You had lunch with my husband?' She shook her head disbelievingly.

'He rang up. I needed to know why you told me he was dead.'

'He is dead, as far as I'm concerned — dead and buried. How dare he invite you to have lunch!'

I started to laugh. This was easier than I'd expected it to be. 'Coffee actually,' I muttered through bubbles of levity. 'He's got a blackhead.' Surely Una would see the funny side. No — now she was glaring, her teeth pressing against her top lip.

'And I bet you had a good old time talking about me, picking over my bones.'

Una's bones were so buried in flesh it was hard to imagine their shape. 'No,' I spluttered, shaking my head. 'He cares about you actually.'

'Oh, come on. He cares about his bank account. He'd rather fuck the business pages than a proper woman. What did he say about me? What did you talk about?'

I don't recall rising from my chair but somehow we were both standing beside the table, facing each other like wrestlers in a ring, poised for confrontation. Sheree's bedroom door had swung open too quietly and we were parted unexpectedly by the swollen shape brushing past us with her head down. She plonked herself in the burgundy armchair and gazed at us questioningly, waiting for something to begin.

Nothing began. Something seemed to end. Una's shoulders sank below her dangly earrings and I took a deep breath that became a sigh. A smell of charred gravy bloomed behind the kitchen bench.

'Oh!' Una ran to the oven. 'Damn. I've done it again, haven't I? That's your fault anyway, not mine. We're both disasters. I don't think it's quite ruined.'

I tilted my head and looked sceptical. I was glad to be spared the overflavoured, clumsily herbed offering and soggy potatoes.

'No, it's all right. I'll just add a bit of curry — that should do it.'

'I've eaten,' Sheree said defensively. 'So what was the fight about?'

I woke with a start in the middle of the night because something was prodding my shoulder. The door was open and light from the living room was leaking into the room, across the carpet, revealing a shadowy bulge hunched beside my pillow. The shadow settled and sharpened as my eyes grew accustomed to the dim light. I sat up and reached for the switch. Sheree.

'What? What are you doing?' I felt affronted that the girl should enter my bedroom without even knocking. The fingers prodded me again. 'Don't!'

Sheree said, 'I had a dream. I think the baby's dead. I think he's died!'

I shook sleep out of my eyes and ran fingers through my hair. 'You said it was a dream. There's no reason why it should die.'

'I don't want something dead inside me. It's not moving. I can't feel it move!'

I swung my legs reluctantly off the bed and pulled my towelling dressing gown towards me. I sighed. 'I'll make you a hot drink.'

'Oh!' Sheree gave a small pleased cry. 'There it is! He's alive. I felt it!'

I let out a relieved flutter of laughter. 'That's good then. You see? You were worried about nothing. I'll put some milk on and you can go back to sleep.' I didn't ask why Sheree had woken me instead of Una but I felt oddly pleased and all of a sudden I was looking forward to sharing a hot milky drink. It wasn't until I was stirring Milo into the mugs that it occurred to me to ask the question. 'Are you wondering what the baby might be or have you seen a scan? You called it he.'

'Did I?'

'Do you care?'

'Why would I? It's not going to be mine, not to keep.'

'I think you do mind a bit. Don't you? That would be natural.'

'I'm not natural. I squashed a kitten once — I didn't mean to. I put a cushion on it and sat on it. I was only five.' She pulled a face and the face became a crying mask, tears squirting onto her hands. She held up the teary wet fingers and gazed at them as if startled. 'I didn't mean to.'

'Sheree. I'm sure you didn't. I'm sure you didn't mean to get pregnant.'

'Well, you're wrong about that one. I meant to but I didn't know it would be like this. I wanted something of my own, eh? I didn't dare tell his mum at the funeral, she was religious.'

'What do you mean, "like this"? What's it like?'

'You know. Cramps in my belly and everyone getting at me.' She shrugged. 'I didn't know stuff that I know now. Tyler didn't tell me anything. He knew things but he didn't tell me — just went on and on about his own stuff.'

'It's a lot to take in when you're sixteen. But you're sure about giving it up for adoption, aren't you?'

'I should be, I've had enough talking. Blah blah blah. Don't tell Una I woke you up.'

'Why not?'

''Night.' She tilted her head in a farewell gesture. 'Thanks.'

I got back into bed but couldn't sleep immediately. I'd been in the deepest dream state when Sheree woke me and now I was really tired but I couldn't climb back into the dream. I was thinking about Sophie and nights when, as a teenager, she had woken me from sleep, round eyes whirling with nightmare images, needing comfort and cocoa. She had been a bit younger than Sheree but way off her first sexual relationship, or at least so far as I'd been aware. And there was still no hint of a grandchild. Women waited longer these days — there were so many more things for them to do with their lives, activities that bound them to desks and cellphones and car seat belts. When had I last heard from Sophie? I didn't like to count the calendar months: it seemed such a mean thing to do when I was glad that Sophie had a life that absorbed her. I'd brought her up to be independent in those far-off days when I was important to my family. I missed that feeling now. I was a cog in a wheel perhaps, at work, at home, but any other cog would help it turn as easily. Really, I was nothing. Was this how Sheree felt?

On Tuesday, one of the days I finished work early, I shared a triangular formica table at the Deluxe with Beryl and the teenager. It was among Sheree's favourite coffee places apparently and right next door to the Embassy, where we'd attended a Harry Potter movie.

'So what did you think?' I asked Sheree.

'Yeah. I liked the flying car.'

'You've read the book?' Beryl asked her.

'I saw the first movie, in Sydney.' She was sucking iced coffee through a straw and peering over Beryl's shoulder at a wall exhibiting tiny paintings that looked faintly pornographic. 'Shit. Would you want something like that on your bedroom wall?'

'Somebody might.'

'Kids!' Sheree complained when a child at the adjacent table started to wail. 'That's the trouble with afternoon movies.'

'Well, it's for kids, isn't it. It's a kids' movie.'

'But you liked it,' Sheree said defensively.

'I loved it,' Beryl said. 'I like to see kids enjoying themselves. Don't you?'

'Nope. Not really. But it was all right. Thanks.' She might have remembered that Beryl had paid for her ticket and I'd bought her glass of coffee. As soon as she had sucked up the last of the drink she lumbered to her feet and took her leave. Beryl and I were happy to sit on over our empty cups.

'Poor kid,' Beryl said. 'I wish I could help her — if she'd let me.'

'How? Help her how?'

'The baby. There must be something we can do to persuade her to keep it.'

'Really?' I felt briefly guilty that I'd spent the last few months looking forward to the time when the girl would have delivered her baby and moved out of the apartment. Would it really make life more comfortable? In a funny sort of way I was getting used to having Sheree to act as a buffer between me and Una: I was even getting to like the girl. But a baby — no, not a baby. I was too old for that! 'No, she seems convinced she's doing the right thing. She's so young, Beryl, she needs to get her own life sorted.' There was a baby in a pushchair only feet away from us and the mother was busy jiggling it to frustrate fitful cries. 'See? She'd never cope with that.'

But when Beryl frowned and shook her head it was as if she hadn't heard what I said and was listening to something else. She was still frowning when the young mother gave up and wheeled the pushchair outside.

'Thank goodness. We didn't come here to listen to that.'

'What?' Beryl turned back to me. 'No, we didn't.'

I was reminded then of Una's comments and decided to bring them out into the open. I explained how Una had gone looking for me at Beryl's house but had felt suddenly shy because 'you seemed to have someone there and it wasn't me. I think you were in the garden.'

Now Beryl was looking startled. She blushed, a process that afflicted her fairly regularly, and then she coughed a little, touching her lips and brushing hair off her forehead. 'Oh no, it must have been the cat. I sometimes talk to the cat — don't you? Or, no, you don't have a cat, do you? Una needn't have run away.'

'I didn't think you had a cat either.' I was remembering an earlier conversation about pets.

'I don't actually. It's the neighbour's cat. I'm fond of cats. I suppose I should get one of my own.' She looked stricken suddenly, as if she'd been found guilty of sounding sorry for herself, playing the part of a lonely old lady.

'I told you about the upstairs dog, didn't I?' I said quickly. 'Slimy little thing, the worst kind of dog — gives the species a bad name. Some apartments don't allow pets at all so Marge is quite lucky.' I took a breath and then added, 'I'm getting on rather well with Kevin, by the way. The downstairs man we tried to flood.'

'That's nice. That's what you wanted, wasn't it? So how well exactly? Has he asked you out again?'

'Not out. In — as a matter of fact.' I made a sound that came out something like a giggle. 'To his place. I haven't told Una so I'd rather you didn't say.'

'But what about Garth? You said she'd be okay with it now, because of Garth.'

'Nothing to do with Garth. Kevin's got a wife — it's a bit complicated.' I explained the complications and confessed how much disappointment I'd felt when he had thrust the details at me. Having revealed this much I took in Beryl's queerly immobile face. 'I guess I'm not a natural adulterer, but I'm learning.' I tried a light laugh.

'You mean you still do it?' Beryl's face was frozen on her shoulders.

'Well — you think I shouldn't? But if it's all right with him . . . They might have some sort of open marriage.' I'd remembered guiltily that Beryl's husband had been unfaithful.

'I mean you still do *it*?' she repeated, altering the emphasis.

'Of course. Why wouldn't I? You do — with Greg. Don't you?' Suddenly I could see from the look on Beryl's face that she didn't. 'Oh!'

'I said he was my friend.'

'And you meant that! I thought it was just what people said — it's hard getting the words right. Oh God, I'm sorry. I've really shocked you.'

'No, you haven't. No, please. I'm just curious about how things work after fifty. My mother told me it all stopped after the menopause. I know that's not quite right but . . .'

'I thought you lived with Greg.'

'I do. Sort of.' She was blushing again.

'He doesn't mind? You haven't seen the Viagra ads on TV?'

'Of course I have. It's not a problem. I'd rather talk about you, Clarice. I can understand how you feel, finding out he's married. But at least he did tell you.'

I shook my head. Beryl didn't understand at all. She was talking as if she believed I'd had ideas about walking down a church aisle with him. Marriage wasn't the point. 'You thought I might be going to fall in love with you? Well, I won't.' That was Kevin's brutal point, protecting himself from the word go, but I couldn't be bothered explaining this to Beryl. I shouldn't have started this conversation. I sat forward in my chair. 'You mustn't say anything to Una, remember? I made a promise. I mustn't talk to her about this because she's in the same building. And she isn't exactly trustworthy, not that Kevin knows that. I only told you because I know I can trust you and you're not a congenital liar. Okay?'

The smaller children had left the Deluxe along with frazzled mothers wiping hair out of their eyes and those who remained were simply young, in jeans or chopped-off skirts that looked like they'd been assembled from the contents of a rubbish skip. A young woman sitting behind us had glitter decorating her cheekbones. 'He's so fun, so out there, so over the top,' she chirped, like an exotic bird. The youth at the counter had turned the music up.

I said to Beryl, 'I can't imagine the kind of life you live

without *it* — as you call it. It's such a big part of what I am, I can't . . . can't look at my life, without getting it in place first. I thought I could but apparently I can't. The sex relationship thing.' I had to raise my voice above the background music.

Beryl glanced about us, smiling through the nearly visible, pulsing rock music. 'They don't know what we're talking about. I hope.' She laughed, inviting me to join her, clearly pleased with herself for being a part of this conversation.

I found myself arriving home at the same time as Una, who worked commercial hours and only occasionally finished later, when she was booked for a skincare treatment. I called out and sprinted to catch up with her while she leaned on the outer doors to the building.

'Hi, Claz. What did you do with the others?'

'Don't know where Sheree went. Beryl caught a bus.'

For no good reason Una sniggered. 'I thought *I* had some funny friends. Present company excepted, of course. But Beryl's a classic. You always had a soft spot for lame ducks at school — I should have remembered.'

'You didn't know any of my friends at school.' We went slowly on the stairs because Una didn't like to hurry and lose her breath.

'You got talked about. Didn't you know? You were so nice to everyone on the bus, doing other people's homework. You were supposed to get somewhere in life.' She didn't add: What happened? But the question seemed to hang in the air above her heavy gusts of breathing.

'I got married instead — is that what you were going to say?'

'Of course not. I got married too. We all got married, it was the next thing. But you had a *brain*.'

'Thank you. But I don't think I like the tense.' We were inside the apartment now, hanging up our coats together in a synchronised movement that reminded me suddenly of the school cloakroom.

'You see? That's what I mean — you know all about tenses and stuff, Anyway Beryl's truly weird. She watches you all the time as if she has to lip-read what we're saying. Is she deaf? And you go to children's movies with her.'

'Everyone goes to Harry Potter.'

'I don't. Sheree! Are you here?'

Sheree was not in the apartment. The TV screen was blank and the kitchen radio silent. This was how it would be in a few months' time when we had the place to ourselves. It was something to look forward to. So why did Una frown while she unpacked her big handbag, placing items in the pantry and the fruit bowl?

Feijoas. 'You like feijoas?' she asked.

'Lovely.'

'Sheree won't eat vegetables, have you noticed? You give her a lot of advice lately.'

'Do I?'

'She won't listen to you so you needn't bother.' She looked up at the clock. 'She'll have to stop staying out so late after dark. It's getting close to her time — she could be early.'

'Surely it's a way off yet. When is it exactly?'

'Like I said, she could be early. I'm responsible, since she's not. She doesn't seem to care.'

I opened my mouth to tell her about Sheree's nightmare, then closed it again. Discretion, something I'd been praised for often enough, was a lonely thing and got lonelier the older you became. I should accept that loneliness was a feature of old age but I was only fifty-nine and I didn't want to accept even that. The other option could have been to transform myself into a garrulous old lady who entertained fellow passengers on a Stagecoach bus, during the cheap travel hours of course. 'When are you seeing Garth again?'

Una's face took on a curiously embattled cast so that she looked more like the childhood self of our school days. 'Do I have to tell you that?'

'Of course you don't. I thought you might want to.'

'I don't know when I'm seeing him. He's going through some stuff at work. It'll be his last day on Friday.'

'I don't suppose they'll bake him a cake. Perhaps you should. What will he do next?'

'The dole, what else? There's nothing else. I'm not looking forward to it — I'll be picking up the tab if we go out and it's not as if we're in love or anything daft.'

I laughed at this as I believed I was meant to.

'Why are you laughing? People do fall in love at our age, as if you didn't know.'

Indeed. I pulled myself up and went toward the cupboard that held the liquor. This wasn't a conversation I wanted to get into with Una. 'But not you — or not with Garth?'

'Certainly not. I'm worth more. Oprah Winfrey told me so. God, I hate all of that love and money stuff. Love and money — it's like alcohol — makes you think you need it. Yes please. Make it a whisky. I'll do the noodles later.' She reached for the drink with a trembling clumsiness that made me wonder if she had stopped at a bar on the way home instead of doing a skin treatment. Or was she going to get Parkinson's? Oh dear. God knows what fate had in store for either of us. 'Oh, he's all right. I shouldn't complain. All his naughty bits work, which is more than you can say for a lot of them.'

'And you've tried quite a few,' I opted for the light-hearted approach, splashing tonic into a rather large gin.

'I have indeed.' She assumed a satisfied expression. 'Even my Roy, if you were thinking of trying him. Don't bother. Roy's French for king, isn't it? He used to tell me that. Well, the king is dead, take my word.'

# Beryl

Beryl sat in the kitchen with the cereal packet between her and the window. She had been too embarrassed to talk to Greg about Una's aborted visit but he seemed to be avoiding her anyway. Instead she munched shredded wheat — rather a lot of it, with sugar. She only bought sugar for Greg but sometimes she slipped and consumed some of it herself. Una must have been lurking behind the fence with her eye to one of the crooked gaps. This arrogant scrutiny of Beryl's private garden might have been accidental but it was no less rude. A civilised person would have called out to let her know she was about to make an appearance. What Beryl hated most was how the incident reflected on Greg, showing him in an insubstantial light and reminding her that this was all he was. He had no more substance than the soft-furred, biddable dog she had liked to think she owned as a four-year-old. Why hadn't her father allowed her a real dog?

'I'm sorry,' she said now to the man sitting opposite her in a shaft of sunlight. 'I don't think any less of you because that rude woman chose not to see you. Sometimes I can't see you very well myself, but it doesn't matter.'

'So when are you seeing the optician? How do you get on at the movies? You'd never manage subtitles.'

'I hardly ever go to movies.'

'Oh, come on. I know you want to talk about it. You should have more women in your life. It's healthy. You could exchange recipes and knitting patterns.'

'I'm not my mother. Women talk about much more exciting stuff these days. They talk about politics. And careers. Jobs with initials. And . . .'

'Acronyms.'

'Thank you. I don't often forget words.'

'You do it all the time.'

'Acronyms and mission statements and strategic —'

'Plans. You forgot again.'

'Oh, shut up.'

'And sex. You can't have forgotten sex? You talked about sex.'

She had been flattered that Clarice trusted her enough to report such intimacies, but sex itself she must have forgotten — in fact she had never quite got what sex was *for*, apart from making babies, and that didn't always work. And although it was all over the place, in magazines, on the TV, even on the radio, Beryl had only a blurred memory now of what it was about — all that fuss. She had known it was important if you wanted to keep your husband — her mother had impressed that upon her — but although she did it with Donald whenever it came up, as it were, she hadn't kept him, had she, so she need not have bothered. Her Mills & Boons, stored in the wardrobe away from Donald, had been her guiltiest illicit pleasure, literally a closet secret because she had read Latin at school and had been ashamed of straying so far downmarket. Part of the pleasure in those stories had been the absence of sex but she hadn't been ashamed of that — why would she be? And these days apparently even Mills & Boon titles had sex. And ladies approaching their sixties. Clarice had thought Beryl had been doing it at sixty-four!

'I don't know why you're laughing,' Greg said, holding his mouth tautly as if he'd trodden on something sharp. 'Are you one of those women who don't know what an orgasm is?'

Beryl screwed her eyes up, peering to see his face better. It had distorted until it was nearly unrecognisable. She shook the sunlight out of her head and looked a second time, staring. First his face flickered and skidded out of focus, then his duffel coat fell away. He had gone again.

*I*t was my turn to run the vacuum cleaner over the floor of the apartment while Una applied her superior muscles to cleaning oil off the sides of the bath. She had left her bedroom doors open wide which was a clear invitation. I advanced obediently with my suction nozzle, humming an old TV theme tune. *He Used To Bring Me Roses*. I was prodding under the low bed, humming, remembering how my parents' bedroom had been furnished with a gleaming chamber pot — the po. There was nothing like that under Una's bed but something was impeding the suction and at once I felt like an intruder, trespassing in private territory, and retreated hastily, pulling back the nozzle which was clutching some sort of magazine. I snatched it off and bent to replace it under the bed, telling myself at first not to look. But Una was no teenage boy, nor even a disgruntled husband who might have appreciated

*Penthouse* or *Esquire*. I found I was looking at a copy of the Mothercare catalogue. *Everything for your gorgeous baby.* Bodysuits. Scratch mitts. My jaw jolted with surprise. Una had laughed at me for buying a koala — what had possessed me? — for the baby and I'd had to hide it in the wardrobe. Shaking my head, I bent down again and cast the rolled-up catalogue to the shadowy far side of the bed.

Sheree had discovered the packets of copper hair colour in the bathroom cupboard and asked me if they were difficult to use. Una came come across the two of us that afternoon positioned at the dining table, Sheree seated with a towel about her shoulders, a smile stretching her wide mouth, while I wielded yellow rubber fingers.

'What are you doing, for God's sake?'

'You know what we're doing. You did it to me last month — you do a great job,' I said soothingly. 'I think I know what I'm doing.'

'Sheree doesn't need highlights.'

'I want them,' Sheree said.

'I paid for the stuff,' I reminded Una. 'We're nearly finished anyway.'

Una flounced — there was no other word for it — into her bedroom and closed the ribbed glass doors so firmly they rattled.

I had tuned the kitchen radio to Sheree's FM music station so that she wouldn't miss the addictive medicine of her Walkman. She reached out and flicked the volume up, grinning and inviting my conspiracy.

I shook my head. 'No, keep it down. She's probably had a hard day at work.'

Una didn't mention the hair at dinner. Celtic copper waves, soothed by my blowdrier, bobbed above a plate of noodles drenched with sauce of a not dissimilar colour. It was after the TV news and *Holmes* that Una finally said. 'You two are getting very pally.'

'What's pally?' Sheree asked.

'Don't you speak the same language as us?' Una asked.

Sheree shrugged.

'Isn't it Garth's last day tomorrow?' I changed the subject. 'How will you celebrate?'

'Celebrate? Hmm. We might do something. He usually goes to the pub on a Friday, but I'm not going there. I might wait for him at his place.'

'You mean like a surprise party?' Sheree grinned.

'No I don't!' Una frowned. 'I can't imagine anything more horrible. And he doesn't seem to have a lot of friends.'

'Shame. We'd have come, wouldn't we, Clarice?'

'No. Not me.'

'Oh! Chicken. I'd like to see where Una goes to for weekends.'

'You want to come?' Una sat up, swinging her legs off the cane sofa. 'My turn to cook tomorrow. I could do it at his place. He's got a dining table now. It's okay.'

Garth had been moving into a new cheaper flat during the past two days and I knew Una had spent part of yesterday evening helping him unpack and arrange some bits of furniture.

I shook my head. She probably didn't mean it seriously anyway.

'Sheree? I'm inviting you. It's only a step away, much closer than his old flat. You could show off your new hairdo.'

'Do you think it's all right?' The girl tossed her hair. 'It is, isn't it? But no thanks, you must be joking. I don't care where your boyfriend lives. He's your business.'

I saw the winded expression on Una's face and winced inwardly. How could two people linked by family be so carelessly nasty to each other? It had been Una's role until recently to crush Sheree's confidence in ways that shocked me. And now it was Sheree being rude and thoughtless. I tried to remember how it had been in my own family, to replay some of our past exchanges, and found a filmy curtain obscuring the details. I took off my glasses and scrubbed them vigorously with the silky edge of my petticoat.

'If you want me to come,' I said to Una, when Sheree had retired to bed, giving her hair a last satisfied pat.

'What? You thought I meant it? Two's company, remember. I only asked Sheree because — well — I dunno really. I thought she sounded a bit . . . She is only sixteen. I should be around when it happens.'

'What about me? I can take care of things, I'm not stupid.'

'You? But she's my responsibility. Anyway it should be weeks yet, no sweat. I mean to have a good time with Garth before he gets the redundancy blues, eh.'

On Friday evening Una didn't come home from work. I found her note fluttering from the square fridge magnet — 'QUAKE-SAFE YOUR HOME' — reminding us that she would be out for dinner. 'Sheree has Garth's address for an emergency.'

'Do you?' I asked her, clearing our plates and starting the dishwasher.

'Dunno. She told me but I wasn't listening. Her cellphone number's in the book if you want her.'

'Not me. It's you she cares about.'

'Cares about? Give me a break!'

'If the baby starts coming. No, but she does care. Why else are you living here if she doesn't give a damn?'

'Beats me! She didn't want to feel it move — I gave her a chance but she couldn't bear to touch me. It was so weird the first time I felt it, like I'd swallowed a whole fish, and next thing he was hip-hopping all over the place. Looks rude.'

'I was nervous when I was expecting my first. I suppose you're a bit scared, are you?'

'No.' Sheree clamped her teeth shut and looked irritable. 'I'll just shut my eyes and scream till it's over. It happens on telly often enough, I'll get through it.'

'Of course you will.'

Una had been away for weekends several times now and I'd enjoyed the break, visiting Kevin downstairs without needing to explain my absence. I was getting used to his sleek espresso machine and only once was I disconcerted when he chose to answer his telephone in the bedroom with the door closed firmly against me.

I'd gone home early that day, leaving my shoes behind me under his bed like Cinderella. I had other footwear. Kevin hadn't come romantically seeking me with a warm shoe in each hand, inviting the three of us to try them for size while a fairy godmother shone hovering in the wings. This weekend he was well aware that I'd be alone with just Sheree but he hadn't phoned. He had warned me that his wife was coming to Wellington very soon but the exact date was still unconfirmed so I didn't like to knock on his door in case I might embarrass him. It was up to him to make contact.

Saturday crawled by so indolently that at one point I stationed myself in front of the kitchen clock and stared hard at the minute hand to check whether the battery was running down. I thought of the expression 'killing time' and wondered how I might slaughter a Saturday afternoon. But when you got to fifty-nine surely you needed every minute there was left. I looked jealously at Sheree's youth and then contemplated how I'd choose to spend my time if I was sixteen today. The idea made me shudder. No, I couldn't bear to be so young and have to repeat all that stuff, make the inevitable mistakes all over again. Could I listen to another fifty-odd years of headlines and global griping? No way. I just wanted the telephone to ring.

I saw Una rolling around on a cheap Belgian rug — the kind Garth would have in his bachelor flat — and sighed, but it was a sigh more self-satisfied than envious. At least Kevin had a double bed, although it was only double because he was double himself, dammit.

The plumbing problem in the bathroom must have resurfaced. The hand-basin cold tap was groaning again, an ugly noise. Why didn't Sheree jiggle it or turn it off? I was about to call out when it struck me there was something different about the noise this time. It wasn't the pipes graunching after all. 'Sheree?' The sound had stopped now and a minute later the door opened.

'What?' Sheree looked at me fiercely from under her red hair. She tugged, straightened a knicker leg under her floppy skirt.

'Are you all right?'

'I suppose so. I think it's started. What shall I do?'

'Oh! Are you sure? Well, that's okay. We're not far from the hospital. I'll ring . . .' What would I ring? A taxi? Or an ambulance? I'd told Una I wasn't stupid and could cope with this, but suddenly I felt insecure. Una's cellphone number was in the book, Sheree had reminded me, but where had Una put the book? And then the cellphone was switched off, predictably. I looked again at Sheree, who was sitting at the dining table now, cradling her chin in chubby hands.

'I'll go and ask Kevin if he can give us a lift. Do you have a bag?'

'No. What for?'

'For the *hospital*.'

'Oh — yeah. My toothbrush and stuff. But it's stopped now.'

'You were making quite a noise before. Was that the first contraction you've had?'

'I had pains earlier but they went away. It wasn't

supposed to happen yet, was it?'

'How long ago did you have the last pain?'

'I dunno. Fifteen minutes?'

We glanced together at the kitchen clock. 'I'll run downstairs and see if Kevin's there.'

'Kevin? Oh — him. Okay. Promise you'll come back.'

'Of course I'll bloody come back. I won't leave you to do this on your own!'

Waiting for Kevin's door to open I remembered his wife and hoped the capable-looking woman in that photograph propped on his piano wouldn't materialise with her high mauve collar and her pretty earrings. He appeared in the doorway wearing his reading glasses halfway down his nose and a knobbly sweater I hadn't seen before. Perhaps it was home knitted, a wifely gift, and she was already there in his kitchen preparing a elaborate dinner. How could I find the time to speculate like this when Sheree was upstairs preparing to 'scream until it's over'?

'You're busy,' I told him. 'Doesn't matter — I'll call a taxi. It might even be a false alarm. Sheree's not terribly reliable.'

'I'm not busy,' he denied. 'Or not that busy. Hang on while I save something on my computer.'

So no wife, or not yet. He placed his hand in the small of my back while we climbed the stairs and I was grateful for the contact, especially when we reached the first floor and found the front door of the apartment standing wide open. I thought I must have forgotten to shut it behind me, but then we heard Sheree making noises again. The girl had powerful lungs.

'You're supposed to breathe when you're having a contraction,' I told her.

'I am breathing — when I get a chance,' Sheree panted. 'Ooph!'

'Are you all set to leave?' Kevin asked her. 'I'll bring the car round. Hadn't you better put some shoes on?'

I went into the little back bedroom to retrieve grubby sneakers from under the bed and shunted them onto the plump feet. I plucked the girl's denim jacket from the coat stand by the door and placed it about her shoulders. 'Put your arms in. The wind's blowing out there.' Sheree complied, something like the child she was, perhaps gratefully, and I was surprised at the good feeling it gave me to be obeyed in this.

Three hours later we were back at the apartment block, all three of us. Kevin had arrived home before us and been surprised when he received my call to return and pick us up from the Grace Neill Block. It appeared Sheree wasn't in labour after all. She had sneaked some of Una's laxative from the bathroom cupboard, which had succeeded in giving her diarrhoea and the beginning of a false labour. She was frightened enough to tell the truth and when the pains had subsided and stayed at bay for more than two hours the ward nurse had decided she needed to free up the bed for another patient.

'Damn. I really thought I'd got it going,' Sheree had said. We were sitting in the back seat of the car while Kevin drove us like a taxi driver. Sheree shivered, hunched into the far corner as if she half expected me to hit her.

I reached out a hand and touched her knee. 'Why are you shivering? You shouldn't be shivering.'

'I dunno! I'm cold, aren't I?'

'You don't have to be frightened.'

'What?'

'That wasn't a very clever thing to do, was it?' Kevin said from the driver's seat.

'It's *my* body.'

'Not your medicine, though. You might have damaged yourself.'

'Who are you anyway? Mind your own business.'

'You could thank him for driving us,' I said. 'Kevin's a good friend.'

'Oh. Is that what he is? I wondered what he was.'

My 'good friend' came back after Sheree had been persuaded into bed. He rapped only lightly on the door and I opened it without hesitation as if I had been expecting him. He bestowed one of his crinkly smiles on me.

I said, 'I'm sorry.'

'What for?'

'Using you. But I suddenly felt helpless. I'm used to having my own car in emergencies and it was like part of me was missing. And Sheree's not easy.'

'Clearly. So do you want to come down for a quick visit?'

'Don't make it sound like that. Better not anyway — I told her I'd be here. And what about — Dell, is it?'

'Dale? Next weekend. That's why I'm trying to get some work stuff out of the way.' He signalled with his head toward my bedroom door. 'That where you sleep? Can I see?'

'I'll make you a coffee, or would you rather have hot chocolate?'

'Chocolate's an aphrodisiac. Better make it tea. A nice quiet cuppa.'

'Really? I don't drink cuppas. You surprise me.'

'Oh come on, let's just go to bed. My place.'

'No.' I filled the electric jug and flicked the switch. 'Where are you going? Not the sofa — she'll hear us talking. She leaves her door open. We'll stay up this end and keep our voices down.'

Kevin poured an extra jet of milk into his tea and drank it very fast as if he couldn't wait to get away. 'You shouldn't have to stay here minding the baby. Does she cut herself?'

'Cut herself? What with. Why?' I was remembering Sheree's flick knife.

'Kids do mutilate themselves. It's a modern disease. As if they could make life any worse — copying what we're doing to the environment, do you think? I thought I saw some marks on her arms when you were putting her jacket on. Didn't you notice?' He put his cup into the sink. Purposefully, as if he were saying goodbye. Then he took my hand instead and pulled me lightly after him away from the main room and into the far laundry alcove beyond the bathroom. The fat washing machine sat with a smaller drier above it at the far end of a narrow cupboard-lined space.

'What are you doing?'

'Guess. She won't look for us in here.' He put his hands on my waist and hoisted me firmly up onto the ledge of washing machine. Then he slid the door shut. 'Make washing machine noises.' He was standing now on the upside-down laundry box, which was made of rigid plastic.

'You'll go through it,' I giggled.

'It's quite strong. And *I'm* quite strong,' he added, pleased with himself. Afterwards he propped his collapsed chin on my shoulder and breathed, pricking me with bristles. 'I said make washing machine noises but you didn't have to take me literally. I'm spun dry!'

We clutched each other, wracked with laughter, trying to swallow it down so that the noise wouldn't flare out of control.

'So much for having a double bed,' I whispered when we were putting ourselves together again, adjusting underwear elastic and replacing the laundry box on its shelf.

'I didn't think I was allowed.'

I edged the door open and we listened together. There was no sound betraying Sheree's presence at the other end of the apartment.

'Don't worry, the coast's clear,' Kevin said, keeping his voice down. I could hear caution returning in his tone. 'The things old people have to do!'

'We're not old.'

'Sssh! Apparently not.'

Sunday evening. I was looking forward to telling Una about the hospital fiasco. Sheree unusually put the tablemats and forks out in readiness on the table, as if she were looking forward to Una's return. We waited until well past the expected hour, then gave in and ate her share of the pizza and salad.

'She's switched herself off again,' Sheree said, pulling a face. 'Why does she do that?'

'Her battery could have run down. She left the charger here — I had a look. Never mind.' But I did mind, curiously enough. And it looked as if Sheree minded too. I waited. We both waited. There was nothing on telly and I found myself regretting not claiming the old desktop computer they were getting rid of at work. Sheree had already given me a bad time about that. The place felt suspended in time, unnaturally quiet without Una's louder tones and the way she flung her muscles into everything she did. She was grumble and shove while I was more placate and apologise, ducking out of the way of trouble when I saw it coming. But now it was Una who was keeping out of the way. Why? I remembered the Mothercare magazine hidden under her bed, which had to mean something. Una had said herself she wanted to be present 'when it happens'. And as the months piled on inches around her middle Sheree seemed to be listening harder for clues as to how an expectant mother might behave. Some force larger than personal selfishness was swelling in the apartment, rather as a foetus swells, ignorant of mental rejection.

At work on Monday, in the glass shell of my office beside the lift doors, I shelved a new supply of dehumidifying capsules for hearing aid users — pastillas secadoras. *Keep out of reach of children*. I thought of Sheree swallowing Una's syrup. Una shouldn't have left it in the bathroom, but what difference would that have made to Sheree, who was free to prowl in all the bedrooms when she was at home alone, as she would be now. Earlier in the day I'd had a disagreement with the young Asian trainee audiologist who criticised my filing methods. It was a minor irritation — I knew my system was unassailable — but the prickly trace of it was attached to the back of my mind like a shingles virus waiting to activate. A departing client wearing a puckered black hairpiece nudged the eftpos machine along the counter and headed for the glass swing doors. It was a quiet afternoon and there was no one left in the waiting room. I lifted the phone and called the number of Una's department.

'What do you mean she hasn't been in?'

'I mean she hasn't been in. Not today.'

'Is she sick?'

'How do I know? She hasn't called. Una hasn't called has she, Debbie? No, she hasn't. Sorry.'

I called the apartment. Sheree didn't always bother to answer the phone, but this time she did.

'Is Una there? It's me.'

'Hi Clarice. No — she'll be at work, won't she?'

'I thought she might have gone home. Don't worry.'

'I'm not worried. See you later, will I?'

'Mm. I might be a bit late but I'll be home for dinner, yes. Tell Una if she gets there before me. Are you okay?'

'I haven't swallowed any more stuff.'

'Of course you haven't.'

I left work and crossed the road to catch a bus to Newtown. I'd decided to visit Beryl and bugger the woman's reluctance to expose her shabby home. It was Beryl or Kevin and I didn't want to bug Kevin again when he was busy before the formidable wife's arrival. The bus drove jerkily, laden with early rush-hour travellers. I lurched in the aisle, flinging a hand onto a window to save myself; beyond the hand I caught sight of Beryl walking determinedly in Adelaide Road, in the opposite direction. 'Damn.' I leaned a finger on the bell cord and prepared to get off.

I caught up with her outside the liquor store.

'Where are you off to?' I heard a whiff of accusation in my tone and tried to smooth it away. 'Sorry. You're allowed to buy grog if you want to. I'm just curious. I was actually on my way to visit you but then I saw you from the bus . . .'

Beryl was looking startled. Then she gave her grey mop a shake. 'I'm not buying grog. I was coming to see *you*!' And she gave a grunt of laughter. 'I thought Monday was one of your early days.'

'Not very early. I finish at four today. Anyway I'm glad I caught you — what a bit of luck!'

'Yes!' Beryl nodded with unexpected fervour. 'And how's the little mother?'

'She's not a mother yet!'

'Well, that's how I think of her. I'm so envious.'

'You wouldn't want to do it at your age,' I laughed. 'I certainly wouldn't. I'm not sure she wants to do it either.' And as we walked together beside the swooping traffic I told Beryl something of the trip to the hospital and the anticlimactic return home. I presented it again as a funny story, a piece of entertainment. It struck me it wasn't only with Beryl that I chose this approach, almost as if I thought people would despise me if I presented my own feelings cold, without a dressing of humour. I didn't, however, tell the funnier story of sex in the laundry cupboard with my downstairs lover.

Sheree had the kitchen radio blaring. We could hear it as soon as the lift doors parted.

'Where are your earplugs?' I shouted so that the girl turned and jumped. I leaned across her and turned the radio so low it might as well have been switched off. 'No Una yet?'

Sheree looked at the clock and shrugged.

'She wasn't at work. She must still be at Garth's place, I can't imagine why. He must have got himself sorted by now. Have you remembered where he was shifting to?'

'I've never been there,' the girl reminded me.

'But she said she'd given you his address.'

'Not that I know of.'

'For an emergency, she said.'

'Oh yes. Well, I must have forgotten to write it down. It's not an emergency.'

'She should have been at work. Perhaps something's happened.'

Beryl was looking about her uneasily, waiting to be invited to sit down. 'Is Una really missing?' She propped herself awkwardly on an arm of the burgundy chair.

'Make yourself comfortable,' I said but at the exact moment Sheree slid into the wine-red cushions. Beryl moved herself off to the sofa. 'I'll put the jug on. No, she's not exactly missing. It's nothing to do with us how she spends her time. But . . .' I continued after a pause, 'it's just useful knowing how many people will be here for dinner.'

'Oh please!' Beryl started up as if someone had prodded her in the back. 'Don't think I came expecting to be asked! I'm just here for a quick visit. Really.'

'I didn't mean you. I was only thinking of Una. No, it would be nice if you stayed. Yes, please stay.'

While Beryl and I sat with knives and forks at the dining table Sheree propped with her plate at the far end of the room where the television set occupied a flickering corner.

Beryl said, 'Sometimes getting older reminds me of holidaying in Noumea — like a sort of culture shock. You can't quite understand the language, the way people talk, the eating habits. Oh, I don't mean here . . .'

Suddenly Sheree gave a shriek and sent her plate flying from the arm of her chair.

'I told you . . .' I warned.

'It's on the news! I bet it's Garth!' She was on her knees, crawling clumsily to retrieve the plate and the few scraps of food that had scattered with it.

'What about Garth? What's he done?'

'Ssh! No, it's gone now. But it sounded like him.' She was clutching her throat: whatever she thought she had heard appeared to be making her nauseous. 'African wild dogs. They found one shot dead at the zoo and it wasn't the first time, they said.'

'So what made you think of Garth?' We'd left the table to come and join her in front of the TV set. 'Was it someone who worked at the zoo?'

'A volunteer, they said. Could have been a volunteer worker, whatever that means.'

'But that's not Garth.'

'What about all that dodgy meat? Eugh! What did we just eat for dinner?'

'That was chicken — I bought it myself.'

'Ssh!' The advertising break was over and the glossy newsreader reappeared on the screen but she had nothing more to report about the incident at the zoo.

'There might be something on the late news.' Beryl was surreptitiously picking something out of a back tooth.

'I don't know why we're even thinking about it,' I said. 'He had a proper job at the zoo and anyway it was his last day on Friday.'

'So where's Una?' Sheree wanted to know.

'And the wild dog was discovered shot, wasn't it? Did they say it had been hacked about?' I shook my head as Sheree shook hers.

'I don't think so.'

'Not exactly Waltzing Matilda,' Beryl said.

'So where's Una?' Sheree repeated. 'It's Monday.'

'Where do *you* think she is?' I asked her and the irritation gravelled in my throat. 'You're not saying they've taken off together with suitcases of wild dog?'

'I don't know what I'm saying.'

'We should have been watching for ourselves instead of telling you what to think,' Beryl said. 'I don't really know Garth, of course but I'm sure he's not a bad person or Una wouldn't have had anything to do with him.'

Sheree snorted disbelief and I cast her a sharp look.

After Beryl had gone home — she accepted the money for a taxi since it was so late — I went to bed and worried. We had sat around waiting for the late news to deliver a clearer version of Sheree's news item, but there was nothing more: a former volunteer worker was suspected of causing deliberate trouble, very much as

Sheree had reported. She'd ducked her head and smirked satisfaction before rubbing her back and hauling herself out of the armchair to take herself to her bedroom. I noticed she was carrying the baby very low in front and waddled rather than walked. And still no sign of Una. How long were you supposed to wait before someone became officially a missing person?

Punching my pillow to knock these ideas out of the way, I was remembering how sceptical Kevin had been about Garth's job at the zoo. But perhaps Una's boyfriend was nothing but a volunteer worker who'd lied about why he was being given the boot. I saw a rifle levelled below his lumpy forehead and his pale eyes squinting toward a loping wolf-like creature. The man could shoot a dumb zoo animal without thinking about it twice, I felt sure of this. But things like that didn't happen near me, violence didn't play a part in my life any more than rugby or winning at Lotto. Neither of my husbands had pursued any kind of sport and they certainly hadn't owned guns. This was when I remembered Roy, the ex-husband of Una whose telephone number was still in my handbag.

**B**eryl called in at the audiology rooms where I was sitting plugged into my computer. She'd been to the second-hand bookshop close by; apparently she'd worked in a shop something like that one when she was a young wife forty years ago. She came bearing a paperback novel, a sort of thank you, I supposed, for dinner on Monday.

'Goodness.' I stood up, smiling. 'I don't suppose you're having a hearing test.'

'No, although perhaps I should be.' She'd held out the book, still in its crumpled paper bag. 'I thought you might like something to distract you — it's not a bad read. I buy a lot of books at that shop and then I sell them back again. Oh, but you can keep that one. I want you to.'

'That's thoughtful. Thank you.' I glanced briefly at the book. 'It's all about recycling these days, isn't it?'

'Yes — actually you're right. Even the plots. Recycled.'

I laughed, surprised. 'I didn't mean that. I haven't done a lot of reading lately, so I wouldn't know.'

'Still nothing from Una?'

I shook my head and had to turn away as a client claimed my attention. 'Don't go. I won't be a sec.'

It was Wednesday. Yesterday on the answerphone I'd found a haughty message from Una's department store pointing out that she would need a doctor's certificate if she stayed away much longer before returning to work. I remembered then that I was going to ring Roy, the husband with a face like junket. He'd been unhelpful, which didn't surprise me, but he'd taken my work number in case he thought of somewhere she might possibly be. This afternoon he'd telephoned suggesting we meet. 'I'm at The Jimmy, down the road from you. I often read my paper here — it's below my new office. Would you care to join me?'

'Er — right now, do you mean?' I restrained myself from asking what for.

He seemed to have heard the question. 'I'm a bit worried for Una. I thought you might . . . Can't you get away?'

'Not for half an hour, no. That's when I finish. I only work part time.'

'Oh. Right. Well, I've got my paper, and something I can be working on. I'll wait for you. Okay?'

I told Beryl some of this while I was closing down my computer and sorting the last of some papers.

'Where's The Jimmy?' she asked me. 'It sounds a bit rude.'

'Rude?'

'Like Jimmy Riddle — Cockney for piddle.'

I gave a puff of laughter. 'Trust you to know something like that.'

Beryl looked gratified.

'It's where Una and Garth had their first date, funnily enough. I think that's the only reason I'm meeting him. He can't have anything useful to tell me.' I looked doubtfully at Beryl. 'I'd ask you to join us but . . .'

'Oh no, I wouldn't. But let me know what happens. I'd appreciate that. Sheree must be worried sick.'

Sick? No, not sick, I thought. It was a word to conjure with just the same. I remembered telling Una in those early days — not very seriously — that I believed Sheree was certifiable, and the look that closed Una's face when she heard the word came back to me now. 'Not certifiable,' Una had frowned, as if it mattered. She was funny about mental illness, hoarding details of her own depressive moods jealously as if they were too precious to share. Didn't she know I was as neurotic as anyone else and not immune to my own feelings of despair?

Outside on Courtenay Place the rain was falling quite heavily now. Two sad-faced old women were on the pedestrian crossing, under half-collapsed umbrellas that flapped in the wind. The bus shelters milled with sodden commuters. I saw Beryl onto her bus and applied two quick strokes of lipgloss before retracing my steps towards the St James Theatre foyer. In a shop window I caught sight of myself with draggles of damp hair plastering my forehead. Not that it mattered what I looked like for Roy — 'the king is dead', I remembered. It wasn't impossible that Una might be drinking there herself.

'It's not that I've had any useful ideas,' he said when he'd bought me the single gin and tonic I'd requested. 'But I thought you should be aware she's tried to do away with herself before this. Did I tell you that?'

'Oh no! No, you didn't.' I was startled. 'But it doesn't surprise me. Not much I can do about it, though, when we don't know where she is.'

'It occurred to me . . .' He stopped and looked at me with a sudden focus of interest I hadn't been aware of last time. He was observing me as a person in my own right, perhaps even as a woman. Goodness. Could he see by looking at me so searchingly that I did stuff like that in the laundry alcove with Kevin? I felt a faint blush beginning on my forehead and moving down my cheeks. He said, pulling a serious face, 'I just hope she's set up automatic payments or direct debits, so you don't get left in a mess.'

'What?' He'd shocked me. 'Is that all you can think of? *Money?*' I pushed my glass away, disowning it. 'I've got to go.'

'What's up? What have I said?'

'I've got to get back. I might be needed at home.'

'Let me give you a lift. It's raining.'

When I reached the apartment one of my soft boots

was squelching; it had developed a leak while I splashed through puddles. My head was hunched inside the moist hood of my coat. Perhaps I should have let him drive me. No, I was glad to have turned down his offer. He was a creep. I'd squelched up to the second floor and was jiggling my badly behaved key in the lock when the door suddenly sagged inward and a strange woman was standing looking at me. My head was so occupied by Una that at first I imagined this must be one of her friends, but then the woman's features distorted slightly until she was somehow familiar. Where had I seen this face just recently?

On Kevin's piano.

'Oh! Hello,' I said, before I realised I wasn't meant to recognise his wife. And a moment later it ceased to matter when I looked past her and heard Sheree making noises similar to the ones she'd entertained us with the previous Friday. 'Sheree?'

Kevin had followed me into the apartment — he must have been only a few steps behind — and now he nodded at me without smiling. 'She's started again. We think it's real this time — don't we, Dale? Dale, this is my neighbour, Clarice. I just brought the car round.'

I approached Sheree, who was wearing Una's rain-proof jacket and holding onto the back of her favourite chair, rocking slightly. She didn't seem to want to let go.

'We'd better get moving,' Kevin raised his voice. He indicated the cheap plastic zip bag that slumped pinkly against Sheree's ankle and I reached down to pick it up.

'Are you coming with us, Clarice?'

'Yes! She's coming,' Sheree shouted.

'Of course,' I agreed. 'I'll just change my coat and get a towel.'

'A towel? That's a new one,' Kevin raised his eyebrows. 'What for exactly?'

'I'm wet!'

'Oh, sorry. You don't have to come,' he said to his wife.

'I certainly don't. I'm jet-lagged.'

'Yes. Sorry,' he repeated. 'I shouldn't be long.'

The rain was easing now but the traffic was building on the main bus route. When I took off my glasses to wipe them clear of raindrops the headlights of the car on the road ahead of me splashed and diffused. Sheree wasn't exactly holding my hand but her fingers clutched at my wrist intermittently.

'Jesus,' Kevin complained from the front seat.

'Rush hour,' I agreed.

'I'm just so glad you turned up,' he threw at me over his shoulder. 'Is she all right?'

'She' was emitting a low continuous moan punctuated with gasps.

'Just think,' I told her. 'It'll be all over soon. They'll give you something for the pain. And at the end of it . . .'

'A baby?' Sheree yelped. 'Jeez, I hope you're right. Feels like an elephant. It'll be a monster anyway. I just want it out.'

'You might feel very different when it's over.'

'Too right I will! I'd better!' She held onto her stomach as if she was trying to push it away from her. The contractions had abandoned her for the time being and she breathed normally.

'What do you mean — monster?' I probed, in the lull.

'Killer genes. *You must know*. Tyler's granddad went to prison, didn't he? Una's ex. And then Tyler . . . He said he'd be in hell and I believe him. That's where he'll be. Oh shit!'

An ambulance plunged by, pulsing with alarming noise, as Kevin turned into the hospital entrance and nosed about looking unsuccessfully for a park.

'I might have to just drop you off,' Kevin said, pulling a face of apology as a four-wheel drive vehicle claimed the parking space he had been heading for.

'Oh shit!' Sheree shouted again, accidentally pressing her finger on the electronic device that opened the window. 'What you gawping at?' This was delivered to a passing couple who had turned with a look of concern.

I marvelled at the girl's lack of interest in the spectacle she was making of herself. I rested a light hand on her shoulder and imagined I felt powerful currents quivering under the warm skin.

'I'm having a baby, aren't I! You're allowed to make a fuss.'

A car was backing out in the path of Kevin's progress and a vacant space appeared fortuitously. He drove into it and turned to see how we were coping in the back seat.

Sheree tumbled herself out of the car and leaned her forehead against the rear door with her feet placed clumsily wide apart. I came around to take her coaxingly by the arm. Kevin checked that the car was locked and moved to join us. He had the pink zip bag, which I'd forgotten, under his arm.

'Thank you,' I said. 'Thank you very much for being there.'

'She didn't leave me much choice. But that's okay.'

'Could you please stop talking!' Sheree raised her voice. 'I could be giving birth to goodness knows what. I'm really scared.'

'You don't have to be scared.' I exchanged a glance with Kevin. Look what women have to put up with. He shifted uneasily, getting ready to make his escape. 'People do this every day — give birth. You're young and strong.'

'I don't want to do this. Here it comes again! It could be a murderer in my belly. Una said.'

'Oh God. Did she really? But you know that's nonsense. You can't believe that.'

A smiling young nurse with very white teeth bore down on us, waving a ballpoint pen. 'Hello there. Looks like you're in a hurry, dear. What name was it?'

'Who the fuck cares?'

'We care very much, believe me. Name?'


Kevin had gone home to his jet-lagged wife and I was allowed, compelled, to accompany Sheree into the delivery room. She seemed to want me there but made little sign that she was grateful. She was busy, of course. Sitting behind my mask — there had been a case of MRSA on the ward — I tried to say the right things to encourage Sheree in her noisy labour, but the right things came out all wrong and sounded faintly ridiculous. In a way I was glad of the mask to hide some of what milled inside my head, but perhaps this flap of cotton filtered communication and censored out reality. Somehow I was there in Una's place, reliving my own birth experiences that had been in another century and no doubt I'd sentimentalised them quaintly. Nothing sentimental about the way Sheree was behaving, bossing the Indian doctor about. He had stopped in for only a moment and cast a sympathetic grimace at me as he left. Perhaps he believed I was the girl's mother.

Would Sophie have to go through this in Berlin, perhaps, without me in attendance? I'd go over of course, if I was asked. Like a shot. Why wasn't Sophie pregnant? Chlamydia or selfishness? Didn't my daughter know how fertility declined as the clock ticked?

'You're doing really well,' I said.

'How would you know?'

I wouldn't bring up Una's name. I didn't want Sheree to repeat that crazy stuff about carrying a murderer in her womb. How could the woman say such a thing to a sixteen-year-old? And why? Supposing that Una had actually said the words. Lies, lies, lies. How did you choose what to believe?

The young doctor had come back and things were moving along. I gulped, choking behind my mask and felt tears spilling down onto the white rim of the cotton. No one would hear me with all the noise going on, so I sniffed and sniffed, tasting salt. And moments later, blinking so that my eyes cleared, I witnessed the tiny form patterned with lacy mucus sliding free into the man's dark hands.

Plunging the back of one wrist across my eyes, I gave one last sniff and stepped forward. A little girl with eyes sealed tightly against the world. Sheree had reproduced herself and she was jerking with hiccups of laughter as if she had told the funniest story and expected everyone to join her in the joke. I didn't want to laugh but my lips had peeled open in an involuntary smile that was almost a grin. My reaction had taken me by surprise. It wouldn't have been surprising if it were Beryl gulping with emotion, but I wasn't Beryl. In fact Beryl should have been here in my place: she'd have done this much better than me. Or Una — no, perhaps not a good idea for Una to be present spreading messages of doom, an evil fairy at the celebration.

'Looks like me,' Sheree announced with a note of satisfaction. 'Not him, anyway.' She was holding the child where the nurse had placed her against her chest, and stared, puzzling down at her for a few seconds. Then she handed the bundle back and watched while the nurse weighed her in the scrap of blanket. 'Good. That's it then. You can go now,' she said to me. 'Where's my bag? Thanks.'

'You should sleep,' I agreed. 'She's lovely. Well done.'

Sheree didn't answer or even turn her head. Her eyes were shut, like the baby's. The nurse was searching for something in the pink zip bag and the new little animal squirmed mewing in the hospital cot. No one was looking to see me raise a hand that wobbled slightly, in farewell.

A curious numbness encased me as I walked down through the hospital grounds, grateful that it was no longer raining. When I reached the main road I stopped walking, slowed to a statue. Something had frozen my mind processes so that I couldn't for a moment think what to do next or where to go. A baby had been born and would go on to have a life. Fifty-nine years ago I began this way. So what? The apartment was just streets away and I had only to turn right and keep walking. Suddenly I was cast back in time to the house I lived in when I was pretending to be happy with my children and a temporary replacement husband — a house with a front and a back door and a rockery and a gate. I remembered it as a comforting memory, a cosy family photograph. But if I'd never existed it would hardly matter. I hadn't done anything special with who I was. How could I feel so much more real and worthwhile than Beryl — let's confess, I did feel that way. But how were Beryl and I different? Beryl had few friends but who did I have? In thirty years I might be dead and what would I have been doing wasting a life when someone more worthy could have lived mine. Hang on, Clarice. I deserved to live. My children would say so. I was kind to other people on the whole. Una had laughed at me for finding lame ducks, but Una was another lame duck: she seemed to have missed that fact, and now she'd swum off, looking for worms. Or perhaps she'd found one.

The apartment would be empty unless Una had decided belatedly to come home. Kevin had his wife sleeping in the bedroom immediately below. She would look up at the ceiling I'd contemplated the first time I borrowed that bed, and her husband. Was the same spider watching them? Bugger it.

The statue I'd become shook itself. I hitched my handbag onto my shoulder and turned left, toward Beryl's street.

# Beryl

Beryl cut herself when she was dicing pumpkin to add to the pork stirfry. She had been making an effort to eat sensibly and restore herself to the modern world Clarice appeared to inhabit so easily. Lately she had noticed Greg Preston changing his habits in a way that unsettled her, making her wonder if she might be going mad after all. It was okay to have an imaginary friend, but why now did he choose to converse with her only in the mirror, peering down over her shoulder, in shadow save for the lightly clenched teeth and narrowed blue eyes? She and a school friend had played a Halloween game as children, holding up a flickering candle at a dressing-table mirror to evoke the reflection of a future husband in the glass. It had never quite worked until today, and today it was no future husband gazing at her but only Greg, a shadowy television image. Yet she could hear his voice as clearly as ever.

The hall mirror was the best, the tallest and widest, although it wasn't so well lit. The swirly patterned glass panels at the side of the front door lent something mysterious to the hall lighting, even at night when the street lamp reached in.

'Shouldn't you have put disinfectant on that?' Greg asked her later when she stepped aside on her way from the bathroom cupboard. She had knocked her hand so that the cut started bleeding again and needed a plaster.

An echo of her mother's advice when she was a child. She couldn't understand what she was doing being sixty-four years old. How could she have come so far from her youth? It must be a mistake. 'It was only bleeding a bit.'

'You have to be careful as you get older. Wounds tend to take longer to heal. Haven't you noticed? Sometimes they never heal at all and turn into gangrene.'

'I don't believe it. I hardly felt it when the knife slipped.'

'Liar. You just forgot it quicker. You're getting older. Little wounds don't matter as much. Don't think you're going to forget the old wounds so easily.'

'That's not true either. I am forgetting. I haven't thought about Donald, not a scrap, not for weeks. And I don't think about my babies, or . . . not like I used to. I don't!' She had raised her voice. 'I don't! Oh go away!'

That was when she turned and saw the shadow on one of the front door panels. It was a real person. It was Clarice.

'I'm sorry, I shouldn't have called at this hour. I wasn't going to knock but then I heard you on the phone . . .' I looked down the hallway, puzzling. Behind Beryl, who was clad in pyjama trousers and a chunky jumper, the passage narrowed, furnished with a low wooden chest and a spindly table that bore a shallow pot pourri bowl but nothing else. No sign of even a cordless phone, so who was she talking to? 'And you were going to bed.'

'No, no. Please come in.'

'I'm not disturbing . . . anyone else?' I glanced past Beryl, thinking of Greg, the aging boyfriend, but not prepared to ask and make a fool of myself.

'I was just going to have a bedtime drink. What can I offer you?'

'I've come from the hospital. Sheree had her baby. A little girl. She was very fast once she got going, and pretty noisy. A cup of tea would be lovely. I'm still feeling a bit stunned actually.' I followed Beryl down the hall, past a big gilt mirror. She was walking quite fast without looking over her shoulder until we reached a badly lit living room and the friendlier colours of a 1960s kitchen appeared ahead of us. Then she turned smartly, her face wearing a stretched smile that seemed belatedly imposed.

'A little girl! That's lovely. I'll have to go in and visit her. She wouldn't mind, would she?'

'Well, you know what she's like. You just don't know how she'll be.'

I thought Beryl must have noticed how uncomfortable I was feeling for her tone of voice changed, taking a sudden decisive plunge. She said, 'You must think I'm mad. You heard me . . . I do talk to myself sometimes. It's a bit of a habit I've got into. It's being alone so much. But it can't be healthy, can it? I know it's not healthy.'

I was embarrassed. 'You can do what you like in your own home.'

'Can I? First sign of madness they say,' she laughed. 'Talking to myself. Or not to myself exactly.' She must have seen my eyebrows lift; she fell silent.

'I would like that cup of tea, if you're having one.'

'Oh yes. Of course. What am I doing? I shouldn't be telling you my problems.' She stepped down into the little kitchen and reached for the electric jug. 'What's the news of Una?'

'Nothing. I'm pretty worried about her, as a

matter of fact, but I don't want Sheree to know how worried. That's supposing she'd care if her boyfriend's grandmother took an overdose. But she might. She doesn't give much away.'

When Beryl turned around with two cups and saucers on a painted tray I noticed the short chunky jumper she was wearing had a picture knitted into the front. A city of skyscrapers. It looked like New York. 'Goodness. You're wearing the Twin Towers!'

'Am I? Oh this.' She wagged the knitted top. 'It's old. I got it at the Presbyterian shop. I knew it was America, but I hadn't thought . . .' She twisted her chin, angling the jumper to allow herself a squint-eyed view.

'That'll be a relic now. Hang onto it.'

'I don't throw much out. Do you like it?'

'There's so much going on out there in the big world. Why do we bother?' I drank my tea, which tasted stale.

'Bother with what? How do you mean?'

'I'm not sure what I mean. Sometimes I feel so far away from everything important . . .'

'I know exactly what you mean. I feel far away too, sometimes,' Beryl nodded.

'From New York and London.'

'Oh. Yes. New York. I thought you meant something else.'

I sipped tea, juggling the saucer. Una and I didn't bother with saucers. I considered what Beryl might have been trying to say. Her problems.

Loneliness? 'We could go in to see Sheree together if you like,' I offered.

'I have to tell you something,' Beryl said, shifting her bottom on her chair. 'Well, I don't have to, but I want to. I'm usually an honest person and I can't keep lying.'

I stared at her over the rim of my cup.

'It's Greg.'

'Oh yes?' I screwed my head around, looking to where the bedrooms must be.

'You must have had an imaginary friend when you were a child?'

'No. I can't say . . .'

'Well, it's quite common. Very. I came across it a lot when I was working at the library. There was a little girl — It was quite charming really, the way she talked to her friend.'

'So when did you work in a library? Have you told me about that?'

'And that's what Greg is. For me. Or was.'

I leaned forward because my ears didn't seem to be working properly. 'Was?'

'An imaginary friend.'

A clip of laughter cut the air before I could rein it back in. 'Oh! You don't mean Greg isn't real? You made him up?' I held my breath and waited for Beryl's nod of apology. 'Well, that explains why no sex! Oh Beryl! I'm sorry, I shouldn't laugh.'

'I know it's mad. I know it's not right at my age, but I'm dealing with it. I really am. At least I know he isn't real, don't I?'

'It sounds like it.' I frowned. 'But that's who you were talking to when I was in the porch?'

'Not really. Sort of. It's more like I was talking to myself.' A little shake of her head and her cup settled in its saucer. 'So tell me about the baby. How much did she weigh?'

I walked all the way home. It was quite a step from Beryl's house tucked in front of the zoo. Women approaching sixty didn't often walk these streets in the middle of the night and counting the people I passed on Riddiford Street I realised very few people of whatever age lingered in the lamplight. There was a small group of Somalis helping someone on the hospital steps and over the road a light still burned in a restaurant, although it appeared deserted. Two tall transvestites walked past me, the nearest swinging shiny high-heeled sandals in one hand. I could have phoned for a taxi — I'd noticed Beryl's telephone hanging on the living room wall. I walked, not because I wasn't weary, but because I wasn't in a hurry to get home and I wanted to think.

I'd passed the op shop where Beryl had — so she said — bought the Twin Towers jersey that she wore over her flat chest and her cotton pyjamas. There was no one waiting in the bedroom for Beryl, any more than there was anyone waiting for my own key to turn in the door of the apartment. Could the time come when I felt compelled to invent company, an imaginary friend? Surely not. Beryl clearly was 'far away from everything' but it was uncomfortably close to the way I was feeling myself, almost as if I were dreaming or certainly not wide awake. We'd talked about the new baby and I hadn't liked to suggest that the child might not be there at Sheree's bedside when we called to visit. The arrangement for adoption was still unclear. As unclear as the future for the apartment if Una didn't return and her mortgage payments stopped. This made me think, not kindly, of Roy and the blackhead prickling beside his eyebrow. I swiped my card on the street entrance and mounted the stairs, deliberately suppressing a glance toward Kevin's floor.

There was something different from silence inside the apartment: a faint clicking noise, too irregular to be mechanical, as haphazard as a snore. I cocked my head and switched on the main light with a fierce swatting action of my hand, intended to intimidate an intruder. The clicking sound continued, coming from Una's half-open glass door. When I moved forward and inclined my head I could smell Una: not Estee Lauder this time but something alcoholic and slightly rotten, like spew. Una was sleeping, beached like an unlucky seal, cast carelessly across the bed, one nostril clicking while the other was buried in a pillow.

*I*t was still quite early on Thursday morning. Something had woken me but when I listened I could hear no evidence of life in the apartment. I opened my door to find Una, who stood immobilised, her arms sagging at her sides and hair smeared like seaweed on her forehead, an upright version of drowned Ophelia, but old and fat. She was wearing a towelling wrap over her daytime skirt and T-shirt, seemingly unsure whether to be asleep or awake. When I spoke to her she still didn't move.

'Una!' I called again. 'Are you all right?'

She turned then, considering. 'No. Not really.'

'We've been worried about you! Sheree had her baby — a little girl. She's in the hospital. You missed all the fun.'

'Fun?'

'Well, it wasn't really fun, no. So what have you

been doing? Apart from giving yourself a hangover?'

Una walked, stiffly, as if her bones hurt, towards the bathroom door. I stepped out in front of her. 'Sorry — can I have a quick piddle?' Jimmy Riddle, I thought, and remembered Beryl and her invented friend. 'If you're planning on having a bath, that is. I won't be a sec but I'm bursting.'

Una stepped back submissively. She must be feeling really bad to act so out of character: she'd barely acknowledged the birth of her great-grandchild. When I came out, leaving the flushing sound of the toilet behind me, Una was still standing patiently waiting. Her round face looked numb, as if she'd forgotten what she was about to do next.

'It's okay,' I told her. 'Bathroom's free. I need coffee. I'll make a pot — I'm sure you could use a cup. Thank God it's Thursday.' No work.

I'd drunk one cup of coffee from the plunger — nothing as classy as Kevin's sleek coffee-maker — and Una was still ensconced behind the bathroom door. I hadn't hung about to hear whether the taps were running and now I took a quick look down the passage to check that water wasn't seeping again. I had a sudden disturbing vision of Una lying in the bath with her wrists dripping blood and darkening the water. Something was definitely wrong.

'Do you want to talk about it?' I asked when Una surfaced from the bathroom.

She looked questioning. She was gulping at her coffee mug but almost unwillingly, as if she had decided despite herself to do what she was told.

'About what's been happening to you?' I asked her. 'What's Garth done to upset you? You can tell me about it. I won't be judgemental, truly.'

'You'll know soon enough.'

'Will I? How will I know? Oh! You're not telling me that stuff on the news was true? It wasn't Garth who shot the wild dog? You're not telling me that was Garth?'

Una shook her head.

'Goodness, you had me going for a moment.'

'I'm not telling you,' Una agreed. 'I'm not telling you anything. Garth's my business, not yours.'

I sighed exasperation. 'For God's sake!'

'Oh *God*. Who's he? Is he a friend of yours? Lucky old you.' She bowed her head and made a laughable yelping noise that turned out to be the beginning of weeping. Her bulky shoulders shook while she gasped and howled. I put a hand on her arm and stroked sympathy, feeling the powerful muscles contort as sobs pulsed in her throat. It was faintly ridiculous that I was offering my more fragile shoulders to support this big woman's despair.

Perhaps Una was in the habit of hiding bottles in her wardrobe and sucking on them in the middle of the night. Or perhaps it was drugs. I was fairly ignorant about drugs. It struck me how little I really knew about this woman whose face left the apartment all powdery and glistening in the morning and sometimes came home greasy with layers of orange-tinted make-up.

She stopped sobbing, wiped her nose on her towelling sleeve and looked up at me. 'You won't want to hear what I could tell you. I'm glad Sheree's not here.'

'I'm going to go in with Beryl to visit her this afternoon,' I said, when Una had continued to offer little that made any sense. 'Come with us. She'll be relieved to see you, I know.'

'I can't.'

'What do you mean, you can't?'

'The things I've said to her . . .'

I remembered. Sheree had been carrying killer genes in her womb. An awful thing to say to a pregnant young girl. 'But if you didn't mean what you said . . .'

'I did mean it. But it doesn't matter, does it. There's no difference really.'

'Between . . . ?' I prompted.

'Killers and . . . and nice people!' She threw her head back suddenly, choking on gusts of laughter. 'Nice people!'

I was frowning, trying to understand. How was it that I always ended up with nutty individuals, women with problems and needs so different from my own they made no sense? I might read faces badly sometimes but I'd always liked to think of myself as compassionate, helpful. Could there be something wrong with compassion, something paradoxically self-indulgent and weak?

'Nice people like you and me. We'd never do anything outrageous, would we, not like my Lachlan, may he rot, who tried to destroy my family, who did unspeakable things to my mother and drove my Jane away from me to

America and someone weird she calls Jesus Christ. Jesus Christ! I mean!'

I restrained myself from opening my mouth to comment, in case I might interrupt the flow. Perhaps it would all come out now.

'We wouldn't do anything like Jane's young Tyler, would we? Shoot some stupid businessman. Oh no. I thought it was the genes — Lachlan's horrible genes — but bugger that. Anyone could do it. People stink. They just stink.' She raised her muscled arm and sniffed an armpit. 'I stink. Tell me I don't.'

I moved a chair and sat closer to Una, gazing into her eyes and looking for what might be in there, troubling her. 'Of course you don't stink. You've just had a bath — if anyone stinks it's me.'

Una laughed at this. She sat and allowed me to look at her searchingly. She was probably well aware that, look as I might, I wouldn't be able to see what was going on in her head.

Commanding knuckles were knocking on the door of the apartment, demanding attention. We sat up straighter and looked at each other. Neither of us was dressed for company, but that was hardly the point. The point was Una's expression of gawk-eyed horror. Who was she expecting? I'd not got around to telling her about the grumpy messages from her work associates.

'Well?' That was Una. 'You'd better answer the door.' Her eyes widened further, expectantly, as I went off obediently in my slippers.

It was Dale, Kevin's trim wife from downstairs,

enquiring about 'the young woman'. She was dressed in a two-piece outfit, casual but smart, from Oxford Street possibly, and looked snootily startled to find the two of us in grubby dressing gowns at that hour of the morning. I noticed her earrings didn't match.

'I told Kev I'd call and see if you needed a lift to the hospital. He said one of you would probably be at home.'

'Una's not very well,' I told her. 'That's very nice of you, but I don't think . . . Come in.'

Introductions were effected, but I glanced only briefly at the empty coffee pot while I was conveying scant details of the birth and the woman took the hint.

'So you don't need a lift? I'm going to the airport in about an hour to do lunch with Kev. I could drop you on the way.'

I shook my head vigorously. 'No, thank you very much. We can manage. But tell Kevin Sheree said thank you for yesterday.' A white lie.

Una hadn't spoken while the visitor was present, merely nodded, and now she was shivering as if the opened door had chilled her. She clutched her towelling robe closer, reaching out for the heater switch, then she said in a harsh voice, 'She doesn't know you're fucking her husband then?'

'What? What are you talking about?'

'You think I don't know? I heard you talking on the stairs. I'm not stupid. I didn't expect you to tell me, did I? You're lucky she doesn't seem the jealous type.'

222

I rallied, collecting words to explain myself, but before I could speak Una interrupted.

'You should have let her take you to the hospital.'

'I said I'd meet Beryl by the taxi rank at two.' I glanced at the kitchen clock. 'I'm going to have a bath. Then I'll make us some lunch, okay? You look — really tired.'

'You don't look a hundred per cent yourself.'

I lay in the bath and soaped yesterday and this unusual morning off my freckled limbs. There seemed to be quite a lot of it clinging to me. It wasn't easy making sense of what Una had begun to tell me about Garth. Had he done something to Una or had she done something to him? What exactly had happened after the dinner she'd reported as disgusting? We'd been expecting Una home on Sunday night but it wasn't until Monday that Sheree saw the news item that might have been about Garth. It seemed so difficult to get the woman to answer simple questions in a logical sequence but perhaps this was my own fault for asking the wrong ones.

Suddenly there was a thumping on the bathroom door and Una called something.

'What did you say?'

'I need to tell you — what happened! Just in case . . . in case I run out of time!'

I dropped the soap and slid, searching for it under one buttock. 'Okay,' I called. 'So tell me.'

'Open the fucking door!'

'It's open.'

It was. Una fell into the steamy room, still wearing

her robe. She banged the toilet seat lid down and then flopped herself on top of it. She seemed to glower slightly at me where I lay, cowering shyly under the cooling water. 'You've got quite a good body, haven't you?' she said.

'Thanks.' I put out a hand and pulled a towel down off the rail as I stood up and the water retreated.

'Body,' Una repeated and gave a shudder. 'Awful word. That's what he is now. A body. I left him under the duvet. He was heavier than I expected but I got him there and then I covered his — his face.' She breathed in a shuddering mouthful of air.

*If Garth hadn't taunted her, laughing at her stories, disbelieving her . . . She'd made a career of lying, of course, had enjoyed disguise and deception and concealment: perhaps that was why she'd gone into the cosmetic business. But this time it was true. She was telling him the truth. The bitter truth, so help me God. He should have appreciated that this was a special gift, handed to him because she felt sorry for him about the zoo stuff. He might have expected her to throw up on him when he told her they'd just dined on dog flesh, not necessarily clean. She had to believe him when he was so angry, at the zoo people first, and at himself for inviting litigation. Instead she'd swallowed a retch, put her glass aside and told him about what Lachlan had done to her own mother, who had been drinking innocently with his mate, the man he'd taken exception to — some financial disagreement. Private stuff. Her mother had called her*

*vagina her 'privates'. At least that was what she called it*
*before she became a merry widow.*

*Una was offering something shocking to compete*
*with Garth's pathetic little crime, wanting a reaction.*
*Wanting, needing — dare she admit it — something like*
*pity. She'd never asked for pity from anyone else, so why*
*on earth mad old Garth? Perhaps because she was mad*
*old Una now. But he didn't believe her. Taunted her.*
*Refused to go to the library and look it up on microfilm.*
*Why should he? He'd looked up her Olympic tennis*
*trophies and found no evidence of them. He'd laughed*
*at the little silver cup she'd won at school and brought*
*over last time in her handbag.*

*'So why would I make it up?'*

*'I don't know really. I don't know why you make*
*stuff up. Probably because you're boring. Whoops —*
*sorry!'*

*But he wasn't sorry, and he went on laughing with*
*his big gob wide open so she could count the missing*
*teeth.*


'What are you saying exactly? He's *dead*? What
happened?'

'I did. Me.' Una shocked me then by giggling. A
moment later she was steely serious. 'Goes like this:
he called me a liar. Okay, you think that's funny but
I was telling the truth. And he was laughing. I had to
stop him saying that — stop his mouth. So I did. It was
this round ball thing — a sort of paperweight. I'm quite
strong really. But he choked. I didn't mean that . . .

I don't know my own strength sometimes, when I'm in a mood. He fell back off the chair.'

*His gnarled hands scrabbling. A child who'd misjudged distance climbing a tree. Absorbed in the contortions of his Adam's apple. The shiny round thing lodged below his moustache jolted as if it were a small clever animal attacking him.*

'But I didn't mean him to — well —' She gulped.

'My God, Una!' I was scrubbing myself dry now, blotting myself between the legs, all modesty irrelevant. 'Couldn't you have done something? Called an ambulance?'

'Could I? Apparently I couldn't. Because I didn't, did I? I'm not sure I wanted to, or not right away.'

'So what did you do?' I asked when Una had followed me into the bedroom and was watching me pull on knickers, jeans.

'I told you. Dragged — and then covered his face — his mouth.'

'But after that?'

'I'm not sure exactly.'

'You must know what you did!'

'Piss off! I knew you wouldn't want to hear this. I can't tell you what I don't bloody remember. Of course you'd have remembered every last little detail, smarty Clarice. You'd have taken notes.'

'I'm sorry. I'm just puzzled.' I pushed my head inside a green jumper and shook it down over my cotton shirt.

'Is that all? Puzzled? And what do you think *I* am? Anyway, I've told you so now you can tell Sheree when you go in to see her. I wonder what she'll make of it. She won't be as surprised as you. I wouldn't tell Beryl, but I suppose she has to find out.'

We were sitting at the dining table crunching peanut butter on toast when I said, 'Please come with me to the hospital.'

'Why? I'll embarrass you. You don't want me to come.'

'I do. I can't leave you here on your own in this sort of state.'

'Waiting for the cops to come and get me,' Una nodded. 'I'll be all right. I just have to wait.'

'But they don't have to come. Why should they? How many people know you were there? You weren't exactly a couple. They might never trace you back here. *I* won't tell. We're friends, aren't we? And I'll tell Sheree to keep it quiet.'

Una shook her head and put her face down into hands that were greasy with butter. It daubed her hair and she seemed not to care. Then she held out her open palms. 'My fingerprints are all over the flat. No, someone will have seen us together at the pub — they'll come. You don't have to lie for me — you're the worst liar I know. Anyway I want them to come. I want it over with. No, you go and meet Beryl like you said. Don't worry, I won't sneak downstairs and tell Kevin's missus you've been fucking him. I was going to, don't think I wasn't — as soon as she got here, since you were being so up yourself, not bothering to tell me. Your closest friend.' She gave a quick amused smile at this description of herself. 'But I won't now. Okay?'

'And you won't do anything silly?'

'Anything silly?' Una snorted. 'Me? As if! But no, I won't do myself in, don't worry. I have to know what happens next.'

I cleared the table while Una remained seated, still in her towelling robe. I took a deep breath and went to fetch my coat. Una called after me.

'Tell her I'm sorry. She can do what she likes about the baby — she would anyway. Why would she listen to me? Although she did seem to listen some of the time, usually when I didn't want her to. Trouble is I wasn't that sure myself, was I, and I might have mixed her up a bit. You know I'm a selfish bitch . . .'

'How do you mean — do what she likes? Are you talking about the adoption?'

'There's nothing set in concrete. I might have lied to you — did I? She can't sign anything till twelve days after the birth. Hang on. I've got something . . .' She trundled into her bedroom on fat bare feet and came out brandishing a booklet. I knew at once what it was. The Mothercare catalogue. 'Tell her I might have been wrong about genes. Look what I did to Garth with my perfect bloody genes! So tell her. I expect it's too late but it might not be. You haven't got any hidden grog in your room, have you? I drank everything I could find last night. Never mind, go. Just bugger off.'

*I* walked, narrowly avoiding being run over at the Basin Reserve. I was preoccupied and not in any mood to notice a speeding BMW. I rehearsed what I might say to Beryl, carefully couching what I now knew of Una's few days' absence in a gentler light. Or should I say anything at all? There was still a chance it might all go away. Or that it was lies — imaginary like Beryl's Greg. Una could have been hallucinating: she did have a psychiatric problem, by her own admission. Unless that was fantasy too. When had the world transformed itself into such a slippery muddle of uncertainty? Was this old age gripping me round the throat? I was aware how old people got stuff wrong all the time as if they'd fallen asleep at a movie version of their own life and were getting ready to leave the cinema.

The baby. Think about the baby. Una was certainly

mad to believe Sheree herself had plans for the poor little thing, Sheree hadn't thought ahead beyond a flatter stomach and didn't want to. I did recall the night when she'd prodded me awake, panicking that the baby had died, but that was because 'I don't want something dead inside me!'

If anyone had wanted Sheree's child it was Beryl. Poor sad Beryl, who was waiting for me near the entrance to the hospital drive, looking far from sad.

Going up in the lift I said, 'Una's back. That's the good news.'

'So what's the bad news?' Beryl thought she was making a joke, one of those props in the game of modern life and laughed happily at her ability to play.

'She was at home when I got there. Last night. Drunk.' I added, 'You don't have to tell Sheree.' I was carrying the small koala bear that I'd retrieved from the wardrobe and stuffed into my shoulder bag without showing it to Una.

'She'll have been in to see the baby?'

'Not yet. Still a bit hungover.' I seemed incapable of releasing more than a few words at a time.

A door in the passage ahead of us swung open and a cheap pink dressing gown stepped out, humming unselfconsciously, swinging a drawstring sponge bag on her wrist. The head of the dressing gown turned and became Sheree.

'You're out of bed,' Beryl stated. 'Well! Where's the little one?'

'Hi!' The girl sounded happy. 'Follow me. I fed her

this morning. It didn't hurt!'

'I'm glad to hear it.' There was sarcasm in my tone. And was it usual to breastfeed a baby you were planning to give up? I shut my eyes in momentary pain, remembering the message Una had asked me to deliver, knowing this was impossible, at least for the time being and certainly not while Beryl was listening. And what was I to say? Your de facto relative Una killed somebody and she'll probably go to jail, but why not keep the baby because nurture's more important than nature after all? It was ludicrous. And it wasn't the plan, had never been the plan when Una and I signed the property papers. Except now the plan was all shot to pieces, our peaceful, shared future life choked out of existence.

Sheree was leaning proudly into the plastic cot beside the hospital bed. When I last saw her she'd shown little interest in the baby: *Good. That's it, then. You can go now.* I'd heard of postnatal depression but this was the other way around.

'You got plenty of sleep after I left?'

'Yup. Some anyway.'

'Oh, she's beautiful!' Beryl was nearly in tears, touching the curled fingers and gazing, transfigured.

Sheree looked across, inviting me to share a glance of amusement. 'She's in love!'

'Well, I am! Aren't you? You must be pleased with yourself. Have you given her a name?'

I interrupted, becoming businesslike. 'Una sends her love. She's off colour — she can't get in to work today. But she said . . .'

Sheree pursed her lips. 'I'm not doing it!'

I was puzzled for a second but Beryl understood instantly. 'You're not? Of course you're not. She's your baby!'

'I couldn't give her to somebody else. Una will just have to swallow it. I'm allowed to change my mind. I had this talk with the social worker . . .'

I opened my mouth, then stopped. 'So what did the social worker say?'

'There's some sort of emergency allowance. I'm too young for the DPB but I can get that when I'm eighteen. I told her you wouldn't mind helping me, even if Una wouldn't. I said you'd probably be quite pleased.'

'Would I? Did I say that?' I felt my eyebrows shoot up under my fringe.

'Well . . . wouldn't you?'

Beryl coughed and nearly choked in her impatience to speak. 'You don't have to go to them. You could come to me!'

I shook my head. My nose felt pinched. I could almost hear the metallic tangle of thoughts rattling behind it. 'It's not a problem. Una said something like that actually — she's been thinking. If you want to keep the baby . . . she was sorry she said stuff to frighten you, she said to tell you that particularly. Okay? I don't know how — but we can work something out. Yes. I'll talk to the social worker. Is she still about?' I was so relieved to have delivered this much of the message from Una that the full significance of a baby in the apartment took a few minutes to filter through to my brain. 'Oh bloody hell, I need a drink.

Coffee, I mean. There's probably a machine.'

Beryl sat, frozen into an uncomfortable position, a collapsed mannequin. 'Are you sure?' she asked me, and then to Sheree: 'I really meant it. You'd like my little house — Clarice's been there. It's near the zoo. And McDonald's. And the supermarket.'

Sheree tossed her uncombed rusty locks and laughed gleefully. 'What did I do? All I did was pop her out . . .' Then she put a hand over her mouth, looking towards the sleeping baby. 'I'm so lucky!' She was keeping her voice down now, unusually for her, when she turned to Beryl: 'Thank you, but I'm used to where I am. You can be another nana if you like. Three nanas might be pretty good. I only had one. Could you fetch me a coffee, Claz? I need to drink a lot of fluids.'

I swayed as I stood up. I'd had a number of shocks and now Sheree was addressing me as Claz, which is what Una called me, no one else. Maybe it was a sign of another change, Sheree's altering position in our life, as if the girl were preparing to be another grown-up, one of us, leaving her teenage years behind. Was that such a good idea after all? Oh God. Anyway how would we all fit in the apartment? But, wait a moment — Una might not be there for long.

'Are you all right?' Beryl had followed to help me carry the coffees. 'I can help with baby. Really. If Una gets difficult.'

Difficult. Thorny. Tricky. Beryl had no idea. I shrugged a bit too vigorously and lost a splash of coffee from one of the plastic beakers. 'Thanks. I might — we might need it. Grandma,' I added, wanting Beryl to smile again, at least.

I wasn't in a hurry to get home and neither was I keen to spend time in the hospital cafeteria with Beryl but this was what I ended up doing. After we left Sheree it seemed easiest to give in and be led across the car park. Inside the batwing glass doors an old man was lying collapsed on the corridor floor, attended by an orderly who waved us past when I paused. Beryl had been here before and knew her way about. The cafeteria was inhabited by a handful of nurses as well as visitors and outpatients, one with tubes going into her wrist, two in wheelchairs. There was a queue.

'Life's all about queues lately. I try to remember stuff and it's as if names and words have to queue up like everything else. There's too much of everything,' Beryl complained, aiming for a table that looked out into the courtyard; I followed with the bottles of cranberry juice. I'd drunk enough coffee.

It only occurred to me after we'd sat down at a table smeared with the last customer's tomato juice that cranberry juice was also the colour of blood. Not a good reminder in a place like this. Sheree's blood had splashed on the doctor's white coat, but that had been joyful blood. At least there would have been no blood at Garth's flat, if Una's account was accurate. I was winding myself up to tell Beryl some of the story. She would be shocked but I found I didn't care about that: I simply had to talk to somebody.

'It must have been an accident,' Beryl said and left her mouth hanging slightly open so that the cranberry-stained tongue was visible.

'Must have?' I shook my head. 'I don't think so. Well of course she didn't mean him to die . . .'

'So that's manslaughter.'

'Not the way she tells it.'

'She might have been drunk,' Beryl suggested.

'I'm sure she was drunk but that doesn't help, does it? And what sort of term would you get for manslaughter in this country anyway? Do you have any idea?'

'And Garth shot one of the zoo animals? What with? Did he go to work with a rifle under his jacket?'

'I couldn't get anything out of her about the dead dog. I just know he wasn't working there as long as he claimed he was — she did say that. *Goes like this*, she said, he had keys that didn't belong to him and worked funny hours. His last day could have been any day this month, or earlier. I don't know why there's been nothing more on the news — I don't always get the paper.'

'Didn't he shift house?' Beryl asked.

'That's right, he did. I forgot that. Maybe that's why. He was hiding. But the cops must be cleverer than that. Mustn't they? I've never had much to do with the police. They have to find him before they come looking for Una.'

'Let's buy a paper.'

'Mind if I sit here?' A fat woman in a green overall had plonked herself down at our table and beamed cheerfully. There was whipped cream on her lip.

We walked through the hospital, following the

painted yellow line along angled corridors, past the row of lifts, and picked up a *Dominion Post* at the hospital shop. Then we had to walk further, winding around to the older lifts and the staircase that let us out onto Riddiford Street. Here we sat on cold concrete steps and read, sharing sections of the newspaper.

'I can't see anything.'

'Neither can I.'

'Well, it wouldn't be in the business pages.'

'Do you want me to come home with you? I don't mind.'

I considered. 'I'll give her a call and see how she's going. Oh damn — I must have left my telephone card in a call box.'

Beryl didn't have a card. There was a notice at reception. DO NOT ASK FOR CHANGE FOR THE TELEPHONE.

'Why do they have make life so difficult just when we're getting older?' Beryl wanted to know.

'Some people are young,' I said. 'Some people have cellphones. Don't worry — I'd better just get home.'

'I'll come with you.'

'Best not. She'll talk to me if there's just the two of us.'

'Oh.' Beryl looked mildly offended. 'But you will phone me if you need anything?'

As I passed the carpet shop and approached the apartment block I had a vision of Kevin and his wife lunching together at Wellington airport earlier in the day. They were smiling at each other, sitting at a table behind the espresso counter and fat aircraft were manoeuvring on the tarmac, while seagulls swooped and dived across an oyster sky. No, that was wrong. He was a member of staff, possibly important, and would have his own office — even underlings who might bring him lunch on a trolley, with tiny bottles of wine. It irked me that I knew so little of his working life, or his home life, come to that, while Dale wore her secret knowledge of him as casually as that fine tweed Oxford Street outfit, moving her skirted bottom possessively, confident, not even jealous of his upstairs fuck.

Kevin would have been so much easier to confide in about all of this, about Una's predicament, which was my predicament in a smaller way. I needed a hug, desperately, a big male hug — what was so different about a male hug? I'd been learning quite well how to do without until now. Dale's timing was just awful, but I supposed it had been nice of the woman to offer a lift to the hospital. I couldn't feel grateful. Kevin would hug his smart London wife. Something more like hatred stirred me until I was rattling the keys in my coat pocket viciously as if I wanted to destroy them.

When I opened the door I expected Una to be waiting for me. The afternoon had darkened while I walked so that the apartment was dim with looming dusk, but the living room light hadn't been switched on.

'Una?'

Nothing. In Una's bedroom her towelling robe had been discarded in a grubby mound behind the glass door. I looked quickly to see if the familiar red wool coat was still hanging on the stand but it was gone. I couldn't believe the police had come and taken her in as she insisted they might; it felt too sudden. Yet whatever awful thing happened at Garth's place might have taken place days ago, she'd been so vague. It occurred to me that I hadn't noticed her car on the street when I returned home last night, although it was usually parked around the corner in Ellice Street or wherever a lucky residents' parking space appeared. I should have looked out for it on my way home today. Perhaps Una had driven back to the flat and the scene of her crime as criminals are said to do. Where else would she go? I sighed and picked up my keys again; I might as well go and check if the Mazda was there.

On the stairs I had a second thought. What about Garth's car? If it was registered in his name and the police suspected him of the zoo shooting, they would have had no trouble finding him. All they needed was to locate the number plate and knock on a few doors. That first visit to the apartment he'd definitely had a vehicle; he'd brought his parcels of bloody meat in it and had found a park nearby. Then — horrors, was my memory slipping? — I remembered Garth's car had been sold, of course. There was some fuss about it: he couldn't afford the payments since he was losing his job, perhaps. Una had talked to me about this and I'd happily forgotten the details, just as Una had forgotten the important details I offered about my children. I was no better at listening than Una after all. Poor Una.

On the street I lifted my eyes and saw a couple on the pavement weaving towards me, arms about each other, not drunk but unsteady with shared amusement. Kevin and Dale. They were more or less the same height and fitted very nicely together. Kevin straightened when he saw me and I imagined he loosened his grip on Dale, although they remained linked.

'Are you all right?' Kevin asked.

'I'm not sure. You haven't seen Una, have you?'

'Have you lost her again? She'll be visiting mother and baby.'

I was shaking my head, but I agreed. 'Yes, she could be. Thanks for the other day, Kevin.'

'Yesterday,' Dale laughed. She was too damned happy.

'Oh yes.' It already felt days ago that Sheree had been panting and groaning in Kevin's car. So much had happened since then. Birth and death, no less. I reached the corner of the road and took a few steps up the steep incline to peer through the dusk at Una's number plate, safely parked. So she hadn't driven anywhere. This seemed to suggest that the police had kidnapped her after all, for questioning at least, in a Black Maria or a panda — or whatever they drove in Wellington, New Zealand.

Round the bend in the road Una was walking ahead of me with her shoulders down; I caught her up as she was swiping her card on the entrance lock.

'I lost you,' I protested, panting slightly because I'd had to run the last few yards.

'Not yet, you didn't. But you will. Why do you care? I've got some gin. It isn't Bombay Sapphire, sorry.'

'I was worried. I thought the police might have been. Or you might have gone back to the flat.'

'What? I'm not going near that place — eugh — never again! You must think I'm bonkers.'

I followed the red wool coat up the stairs without disagreeing.

'I had to get a drink,' Una told me, when she had slopped two generous measures of gin and slumped with an elbow on the dining table. 'I've remembered what I did, Claz. Afterwards. It's not very interesting but it reminded me I needed to get this.' She lifted up the Beefeater bottle and her wrist drooped tiredly as if she were already on her way to being drunk again.

I joined her with the bottle of tonic. 'So? Are you going to tell me?'

'Of course I'm going to tell you — keep your hair on. Not too much!' She snatched her glass away so that some of the tonic I was pouring spilled onto the leather tablemat. She drank. 'That's what I did. *This*. Drank everything I could lay my hands on, but not until I'd searched the place for some pills, and the bugger didn't have more than a couple of Imovane. I thought it might be enough with neat gin, but it wasn't because I woke up quite soon after — well, it felt soon after — and I was still there at his bloody table, with the candles gone out. It was weird.'

*Just the stereo monitor and the bright figures blinking on the clock. The room was barely furnished apart from a pile of cardboard cartons, some of them crushed ready for disposal behind the door. The floor rug was disturbed, badly rucked up where she had dragged him to the bedroom*

*— she could see this when her eyes grew accustomed to the grimy half-light from a high window fan.*

'I didn't go back into the bedroom. Neither would you.'

'Maybe he's not dead. Were you sure? Didn't you even check?'

'No! I told you I didn't. But he was dead all right.'

'So you just came home?'

'First I cleaned up the sick. I must have been sick. I could have choked!' She gulped with laughter at this. 'On my own vomit. It happens. But no such bloody luck. And the police didn't come — I thought they might, after that zoo story on the radio.'

'Was it on the radio?'

'But he'd shifted flats, hadn't he? Thought that was all he had to do — silly bugger. They'll track him down — they have to. And then it'll be me. What's worse — one wild dog or one whingeing Pom? So what did Sheree have to say about it?'

'I couldn't tell her. Not about Garth. Don't be silly.'

'Why not? She's tough enough. She has to find out sooner or later what sort of person I am.'

'Well —' I shrugged. 'But she was too happy. I didn't like to bring her down.'

Una raised her eyebrows and then her glass. 'We're wetting the baby's head, are we? I nearly forgot. I'm surprised she's happy — she's going to have to pull herself together. This is where the hard stuff begins.'

'Motherhood, you mean? Solo?'

'She doesn't want the baby, remember?'

'But you said . . . Have you changed your mind again?'

'Mind? That's the trouble with me, isn't it? I'm not sure I've got one. I think I've just lost it, and good riddance. It won't be much help to me in prison.'

'Do go easy on that stuff,' I said. 'You'll make yourself sick again.' I moved the gin bottle off the table and placed it on the kitchen bench. 'Sheree's decided she wants to keep the baby.'

'I suppose you told her, did you?'

'No, she'd made up her mind before Beryl and I even got there. She'd talked to someone — a social worker.'

'But you told her what I said, about the genes?'

'I did. Yes, I told her that.' I was glad to be able to report this without lying.

'Good.' Una sounded pleased, as if she meant this.

I began to tell her about the emergency allowance and how Sheree expected to come home with her baby to this apartment and have three grandmas — or one great-grandmother and two surrogate grannies. And which bedroom would the young mother sleep in — mine or Una's? — since space would be needed for a baby bassinet and it wouldn't fit in the little back room. For a moment I could pretend none of the other stuff had happened and look at the possibility of life continuing much as before, with only minor adjustments. But somewhere during this recital Una had stopped listening, or she was listening to another voice that I couldn't tune in to.

'I'm going to the police,' Una said later, when she woke up on the sofa and saw me moving about, wiping down the table with a damp cloth. It was late. Tomorrow I was expected to go in to work at ten in the morning.

'Don't be silly. What for?'

'I have to make a statement. I need to be punished, don't I?'

'You need to get a good lawyer, that's what you need.'

'I don't deserve a lawyer, and I can't afford one.'

'You might get legal aid — you have to — it's the law.'

'Oh, that's right, you worked in one of those places once, didn't you? Hah. I suppose you know everything about murder, or you think you do.'

'I don't know much at all. Or manslaughter. Honestly, Una, you have to talk to someone before you start admitting anything. If you were going to bring in the police the time for that would have been straight after he fell off his chair.'

She was laughing, loosely, her lips slack with gin and I noticed she must have dribbled while she was sleeping. She laughed almost with pleasure, delighted at my reaction. 'You talk like you were there with me. How do you know so much? Clever Clarice.'

'You told me about it,' I reminded her.

'Oh, did I? I suppose I was telling the truth, was I?'

'I think so,' I frowned. 'It sounded like it.'

'Okay. Yes,' Una stopped laughing and tried to pull herself up straighter on the sofa. 'It was, actually. The truth, actually, so help me God.' She shut her eyes. 'I think I might leave the police out of it for now.'

*I* made some phone calls after breakfast. I excused myself from going in to the office, claiming a migraine. Normally I would have worried that a lie like this would deserve the truth rebounding and punishing me with a blinding headache, but this time it was excusable. So why did my temples throb with a threatening pulse? I rang Una's work as well and lied for her, while she sat within hearing distance wearing an ironic expression — it hadn't been her idea, this lie. Then I called the law firm where I'd worked, oh quite a few years ago now, and learned that my immediate boss had 'passed away a few years back'. I asked for the phone number of one of the law clerks who'd been a sort of friend once upon a time; no one seemed to remember who I was talking about, or even who I was. I replaced the phone, feeling bruised and discouraged.

'I don't know what you think you're doing,' Una

said. 'I don't need anything from you. I'm quite capable of making a confession and getting the sack without any help.'

The phone shocked us. It sounded unusually loud as if I'd accidentally turned up the volume; we started, in perfect time. It was Sheree, calling from a hospital phone. She didn't at once ask for Una — she'd clearly expected an answerphone message instead of my voice — but Una jumped from her chair and held out a demanding hand.

'Hi, Ditzy! I won't say I didn't think you had it in you — you had something in you anyway . . . I'm pleased. I bloody am. Would I lie? . . . I can't. Tomorrow? Isn't that a bit soon? I can't pick you up, sorry — I'm a bit tied up.' Tied up. She caught my eye and began to giggle. 'And I can't talk now. We have to go to the p— p— police station.' She was stuttering with laughter, so that I had to snatch the phone back from her.

'Just to provide some information. Don't worry about it. I'll pick you up tomorrow if Una can't. Drink lots of water. We might be in later.'

Una was looking sour when I turned around. 'You don't have to come with me.'

'Don't I really?'

She bowed her head. 'Yes, please. Please, Clarice.' The humour had sloughed off her face, leaving it creased and pasty. 'I don't even know where to go.'

Una parked the Mazda in the library basement car-park because it was close to the police station and we sat leafing hurriedly through the newspaper before going to feed money into the meter. I was relieved to have arrived safely this far at least. Una had driven — she had insisted on driving, well it was her car — with a reckless abandon that made my stomach clench; swerving sideways to the stationer's on Victoria Street and then having to travel in a circular sweep to approach the car park on her second attempt. It was only luck that saved us from running out of petrol. My long fingers shook as I flapped the paper open.

It was there on an inside page — staring up at me. 'Man's Body Found.' I must have read it aloud.

'What? Where?'

I pointed.

*Wellington police have launched a homicide investigation after a suspicious death. The body of an elderly man was found in the bedroom of a Te Aro flat, where he was a new tenant. Police were alerted to the death by the owner of the property. The dead man's name will not be released until his next-of-kin have been contacted.*

I felt sick. This was it. It wasn't a story, it was true. I leaned my head against the window glass. Reality tilted, then righted itself again.

Una was opening the driver door. 'I've got to find a loo or I'll shit myself. Can you do the meter?' She ran, skipped plumply, towards the lift doors, leaving me behind in the car.

In the library foyer at ground level I stopped, considering which toilets she would have headed for. Upstairs by the coffee shop, inside the library on the first floor? I'd just have to wait by the lifts or risk missing her.

I waited. The lift doors opened and closed, the doors to the library admitted and dismissed men and women of varying ages, with bags and satchels and handbags, untying scarves, pushing glasses up noses, stepping on cigarette butts. Two old women were taking a ridiculous amount of time to get up the wide stairs in the curving direction of the coffee shop or perhaps the Senior Centre. One day soon Una and I would be seniors. I watched, feeling my shoulders sink, my thoughts congeal. Bugger Una. She couldn't be taking this long with a dodgy hand-drier in the ladies. Surely she hadn't decided to brave the police station on her own? I stepped out onto the pavement and looked doubtfully towards the POLICE sign up the road. Unlikely. Then I turned and thought I saw a flash of Una's red wool coat beyond the library information desk. No, perhaps not. I stood impatiently in front of the doors, then passed through, searching. The ground floor was airy and light with deep windows of glassy grey sky. Occasional computer screens punctuated a fanning view of book spines. One of the up escalators was disabled and a group of petulant readers was straggling in the stairwell. I moved quickly, my eyes darting between the low shelves.

A fat red coat had its back to me in front of an electronic book-issuing machine.

'Una!'

'Oh! You made me jump. Have you ever used this thing? It seems to work. Look — I thought I should get myself something to read, I haven't read a book for weeks. You put your card here — I've got my card — see — and then . . .'

'Una. We're going to the police station — aren't we? I've been waiting for bloody ages.'

'Oh. Do we have to?'

'It was your idea in the first place.'

'I don't think so. I think it was your idea. I don't really want to. I'd rather have a carrot juice — they do a good one at Clark's. I don't think I need this book after all.'

I shook my head, trying to look amused. I wasn't amused. 'You're impossible.'

'Well, tell me something I don't know. Or a coffee? You want a coffee, I know you do.'

'Okay. A coffee and we'll talk about it. I'm getting really tired.'

Una mashed her scone with a fork. 'Why do they have to assume someone else did it? Maybe he just decided to put the thing in his mouth. He was mad enough. And he did talk about shooting himself with his air pistol once. He wasn't keen on living without his job and without the stupid animals he thought he could care for.'

'Cared enough to shoot one. Or two,' I remembered. 'It won't work, Una. Fingerprints. You said it yourself. He had someone else's prints on the paperweight. All over the flat, you said.' I screwed my eyes up, thinking. 'And he hadn't threatened you at all. You weren't defending yourself.'

'How do you know? I might have been. I'm trying to remember.'

'Well, that's the sort of thing you need a lawyer for. A lawyer might make a case for you at least. A good lawyer. I couldn't recommend the bloke I used for the divorce . . .'

'What sort of case?'

'There's always unsound mind,' I said.

'Hah! I knew you'd come up with that. *He* was mad — bloody Garth was mad!'

'It doesn't have to be true. *Seen* to be true is what matters. Like justice has to be seen to be done, not necessarily *done*.'

'You surprise me. I thought you were more moral than that. Tell the truth at all times, a good little girl guide.'

'You're my friend,' I said. 'And I'm your friend. That's what it's about.'

She stared at me. 'So you say. Yes, I think you really are. I don't deserve you. And I'm not ungrateful, Claz. I'm not really such a shit, you know, just when I can't help it.' She paused. 'So what's wrong with that bloke the agent came up with for our conveyancing? No, you're right, he wouldn't do at all. There's always the *Yellow Pages* . . . My first husband's lawyer was top rank but Lachlan still went inside and anyway he was an old bloke — he'd be dead. My mother's solicitor's definitely dead.'

'Your mother's solicitor? Why him? Was he good?'

'Well . . . It doesn't matter, he's dead. Everyone

good's dead these days, some of my best mates.'

'And your mother?'

She didn't answer.

'Roy's not dead,' I remembered, thoughtfully.

'Yeah — Roy's solicitor was bloody good, or he said so.' She grasped the change of subject with something like relief. 'I could ring Roy — that would give him something to think about. From the police station, eh? Or *you* could — if you thought you could do it better. You could renew your acquaintance.' Her forehead creased, pondering, then she looked down at the watch on her wrist.

'Plenty of time,' I said. 'The police station won't close on us.'

'But the bank will.'

'What do you need the bank for?'

'I'm supposed to check a credit fund application I put in for. I applied for this extension. No, it's not important.' She glanced at her watch again.

'What now?'

'How much parking time did you pay for? We've been here a while. And we'll need a good hour in the cop shop.'

'More like two.' I stood up. 'We'll have to top it up.'

'I'll do it. You finish your coffee. I've got plenty of change.' She seemed pleased to be doing something thoughtful and sensible. 'I don't suppose you want this scone. It's quite nice, but I think I've killed it.'

I'd been sitting there for a long time — plenty of time

to lean across and borrow one of the stapled *Dominion Post*s with the coffee-shop name inked on it. Time to read again the entry, 'Man's Body Found', more than once. A waitress had removed the dead scone and Una's empty glass while on the shiny wooden table top I turned my cold coffee cup round and round, round and round. At last I got up, sighing, unsurprised, and went down in the lift to the car park.

The car had gone.

The sky curdled so quickly in September. It wasn't late but the window at the back of the apartment was shrouded with dusk that slunk already in the leafy garden behind the apartment. The statue with a broken buttock raised its hand as usual in the tiny courtyard but very soon it would be only one of a dozen shadows, multiplied by the darkness. Two cats were keening lust somewhere out of sight. From another direction a muffler on a car driven by a boy racer was squealing speed. I spooned a serving of boysenberry ice cream from a cup and looked sideways towards the front door, waiting for Una's key. It should have been impossible to feel truly alone so close to the action of the city and yet I felt hollowed by loneliness.

I'd eaten two more servings of ice cream — at this rate I'd be as fat as Una and Sheree — when the door at last moved inward, behind Una's hand.

'So?' I asked her.

'So nothing. I decided there was no rush. I went to the bank.'

'I didn't see you there. I looked. I'd waited ages.'

'Sorry. You know what I'm like. I thought I should get a few things sorted just in case. I might not get bail.'

'Of course you will. It may not come to court for months.'

'And Sheree's coming home with her baby. Oh Gawd.' Una threw her handbag into her bedroom and went to the kitchen cupboard, looking for a glass. She held it under the tap without looking, so that it overflowed for minutes before she noticed. The stainless-steel bench was clear of the mess we'd left behind in the morning and the dishwasher murmured, filling with water. 'You've been slaving.'

'Yes. I didn't know what else to do. There's a casserole in the oven.'

'You haven't phoned Roy for me?' She waited briefly for me to shake my head, then went on, talking rather fast. 'There's a lot to get sorted, I've been thinking. Goes like this: I can clear some of my stuff from the wardrobe, pack the winter things — they'll go downstairs in the storage cupboard, in one of the boxes, or in a suitcase if necessary — and I might decide to put myself in Sheree's room. That would be good for me, wouldn't it? Get me used to a smaller space like a cell. Prepare me for when it happens. She has to have the baby in with her — you said it yourself — so one of us has to move. Oh, I don't mind. And then . . .'

'Slow down. You don't have to do anything in a hurry.' This must be what manic means. I'd seen Una depressed, but never quite like this, or not that I'd noticed. Manic-depressive is called bipolar these days, but that wasn't necessarily the expensive name her therapist had handed her.

'I do. There isn't any time. I think I'll get the boxes right now.' She strode to the row of brass hooks at the back of the coat stand and plucked the relevant key.

'The casserole's about ready.'

'I won't be long.'

'I'll come with you,' I offered, doubtful about letting her out of my sight in this state.

The entrance to the storerooms was tucked under the staircase opposite Kevin's apartment, and while I was hovering in the passage he shouldered his way in from the street, burdened with a carton of wine bottles. He straightened, balancing the box against his front door.

'Hello!' There was a timbre of intimacy in his tone until he divined that someone was ahead of me, rooting about.

'Hi. Una needs to store some stuff. We're expecting Sheree home with the baby, and . . .' I took a deep breath, lowering my voice. 'All sorts of stuff. I can't tell you now.'

Kevin's voice changed gear and opened out into a tone of social conversation. 'Dale's busy with the new breadmaker she bought us yesterday. She talked about inviting a couple of people for drinks and cinnamon rolls this evening. That includes you and Una, of course.

I'm stocking up the drinks cabinet. You'll come?'

Una emerged, dusting a cobweb off her forehead, dragging a mottled suitcase on wheels, while Kevin repeated his invitation.

'Of course we will!' She flashed a smile that was too sudden to be convincing.

'Will we?' I sounded doubtful.

'What? You're turning down machine-made muffins?' Una wobbled her jowls humorously.

This sounded faintly rude and compelled me to agree at once, apologetically, smiling. 'Thank you. What sort of time?'

'Any time. After eight. Like the chocolates.' He flashed his troublesome smile at me as we left.

'Was that a hint?' Una asked, kneeing the suitcase ahead of her into the lift. 'Do we have to bring chocolates? We don't really have to go, do we?'

'You shouldn't have accepted if you didn't want to go. Is that suitcase going to be big enough? I thought you wanted boxes.'

'You can go without me, don't worry. I know you want to go to your boyfriend's. A breadmaker, eh? You could tell she was a breadmaker type, couldn't you?'

The telephone rang while we were eating dinner. Una was barely swallowing any of her mashed potatoes and lamb; she had forked them into separate piles that she pushed about the blue and white plate distractedly. The phone made her start. She allowed me to answer it and kept her head down listening while I apologised to Sheree for our not having visited the hospital.

'She's not coming home tomorrow,' I told Una, covering the mouthpiece. 'Apparently someone wants to talk to you first. The social worker.'

Una grabbed the phone. 'That's crazy. What for? Do they think there's something wrong with this place? Nothing's changed. This was your address when you went in and . . . Monday? Why not tomorrow? Social workers must put in hours even on weekends. I'm busy on Monday. Because I have a life! I'm not your legal guardian.' Then she pulled a face. 'Am I? All right, I suppose. Wouldn't Clarice do?'

'Would I do for what?' I asked when the phone was back on its cradle.

'Oh — I've got to sign something, I think. I've got too much on my mind!'

'I thought you'd be pleased to have a bit more time before she came home with the baby. Brenda.'

'Who?'

'Brenda. That's the baby's name — didn't she say?'

'I've got too much to worry about. I don't know what happens next! Anything could happen. I didn't know life was so dangerous. I don't even have a job.'

'You did have last time I spoke to your boss.'

'No. You don't understand. I can't go back there, never mind bail. Lawyers don't solve anything — its just burble verbal, blah blah. I heard some of the stuff my mother's solicitor was charging huge bucks to spout. Useless.'

'What was your mother's problem?' I asked, keeping my voice low and steady in the hope that Una's voice might slow down to meet my level.

'What?' Una looked at me with a sudden piercing focus. 'My mother? Yes, Mum was a victim all her life — all she taught herself was how to duck and she didn't always manage that. That's not me. Victims get raped, they get their throats cut. She was lucky to die a natural death. You have to stand up and put the boot in.'

'I remember you said she drank.'

'Did I say that? She did, a bit. What else would she do? Poor Mum. She was a fifties wife, she didn't even go to work.'

'But what actually happened?'

Una was silent for a brief minute. 'Don't forget we have to go downstairs for drinkies.'

I sighed. 'You're still not telling me stuff, are you?'

'What do you mean — still? I'm the same person. Just because I killed someone doesn't make me a different person.'

I wrinkled my forehead because that was pretty much what I had been thinking. She looked across at the big-handed clock in the kitchen. 'All right, let's make ourselves presentable.'

It felt strange being in the downstairs apartment, smaller but so much more glamorous than ours, with Dale operating the coffee machine instead of Kevin. She was clearly in charge of the space now and had probably been responsible for the décor as well, including the small weighty bird sculpture that had brought Kevin's and my hands together that first time. Until now the room had never presented itself to me as anything but

Kevin's. Its transformation to Dale's setting caused a sort of physical wrench in my head as if the room had been picked up and shaken like a Christmas paperweight so that the image of my lover vanished behind a swirl of white.

Perhaps the paperweight in Garth's mouth had shaken with an eddy of frozen ice when Una pressed it down, down. One day these people sitting politely behind wine glasses might read lurid newspaper details about all of this, although I was aware that not all murders became public knowledge and had said as much to Una. In fact it was surprising that the Wellington police were taking so long to track down Garth's lady friend; perhaps he practised secrecy as intently as she did. Was it because I was middle class and middle-aged that I couldn't believe uniforms might never knock on the apartment door if Una didn't go to them herself and confess? Crime doesn't pay, we were taught at school. Murder will out.

The murder we talked of with Kevin's friends was all overseas murder: a beheading in Pakistan, fatal white powder in the USA. White for danger. Asbestos, toxic fish, leprosy, white lies.

'Lovely,' crooned Marge from upstairs, waving a cinnamon roll that was singularly chewy, and perhaps reminded her of biscuits purchased at The Warehouse for her little dog, India.

'A champagne cocktail,' Dale was telling Una. 'Brandy and a teaspoon of sugar. Kevin says half a teaspoon is enough and I guess he's the expert. You'll try one, won't you?'

'Clarice would agree with Kevin, of course.' Una was getting a little bit drunk, which was worrying. 'The expert. And she would know.'

'You don't like sugar?' Dale asked me innocently.

'I think we should go,' I stood up. 'Sheree's bringing the baby home and Una wants to clear some space . . .'

'Not tomorrow. Monday actually — loads of time.' She stood up and staggered slightly, neatly elbowing a plate of nibbles off the coffee table onto the mat. 'Whoops. Okay. You're right. We're going. Thank you, thank you, for a lovely muffin and a very — Goodnight!'

When we were inside our own front door and Una had stopped laughing at her clumsiness, she reached out and put heavy arms clumsily about me. She gave me a little warm hug, something we never did. 'Thank you, Clarice. I have to thank you. I owe you.'

'For?' But I was shaking my head and smiling forgiveness.

'Thank you for not letting me get drunk. I couldn't have coped with getting drunk tonight, that would have been a really bad idea.'

I passed Una several times as we were preparing for bed. I kept forgetting things I needed in my room overnight — paracetamol, nail scissors, a glass of water. Una seemed similarly disorganised. When I was fetching the paracetamol Una was busy at the kitchen bench packing a handful of bottles, which looked to have come from the bathroom cupboard, into a deep toilet bag.

'What's that for? Are you going somewhere?'

'I'm going to prison, aren't I? Arohata, I hope, and

not yet, I hope. But you have to be prepared, like when you're booked to have a baby, eh. I told Sheree to be prepared for the hospital and this is the same. I have to be ready, don't I? Don't worry. Sleep tight. I'm just doing the right thing. If you hear me moving about in the night . . .'

And I did hear Una. I wished she hadn't warned me that I might be disturbed — it seemed to keep me awake, listening. There were other things I needed to think about. Kevin was one of them but I tried to postpone that: my turn would come when Dale had departed — but what if she decided to stay? The end so soon? There were too many endings in my life already and all leading inevitably towards the final ending. The last of the series. Sheree's baby was probably a good idea, the best possible idea: she would give the apartment a new light, a new cast. And dammit, I'd promised to ring Beryl, who had completely slipped out of my mind.

Una was still busy, cupboard doors closing — pock, pock — a kitchen stool scraping, curtain hooks — or perhaps coat hangers — sliding noisily on a metal rail.

Because I'd had such a disturbed night I slept unusually late on Saturday morning. I'd woken up in fright, remembering a worrying dream that leaked away even while I was sieving for details; some of the dream residue I recognised as true and belonging to yesterday. Fragile with lack of sleep, I noticed that the kitchen wastemaster ponged a bit — it must have been weeks since we poured sanitising bleach into the torn rubber mouth. There was a magnet on the fridge — 'Mr Muscle — The only man I need in my kitchen'. It was Una's magnet, Mrs Muscle's.

Una was gone. Missing again. But this time it seemed more serious. The mottled suitcase on wheels was no longer in the bedroom and the toilet bag she had been packing was doubtless inside it now, wherever it was, bulging with the contents of Una's bathroom shelves and her battery electric toothbrush.

In Sheree's room nothing had been disturbed; her poky wardrobe had always been half empty — the girl owned so little. Several items of Una's clothing remained hanging in her wider bedroom wardrobe, but they'd been shoved to one side, hems sagging, zips ruptured, buttons dangling, unloved and unwanted. There was something horridly final about the stripped wardrobe and vacant drawers, half closed. She had left in a hurry, a burglar who had burgled only her own belongings, so far as I could tell. Una's heavy arms hugging me — 'I owe you' — spoke to me with a new force in the morning sunlight.

I was grateful for the autumn sunshine at least. Una's ornamental giraffe watched me with red-eyed indifference, abandoned like her dog-eared clothing. I wondered whether Garth had known of the creature's existence in the apartment. I'd hated it when it moved in, occupying too much space beside the sideboard. It was the same kind of hostility I'd felt toward Sheree in the early weeks, but I didn't really mind the giraffe now. I noticed the rain jacket that Sheree liked to borrow had been left behind, perhaps thoughtfully. In fact there were plenty of Una's possessions still decorating the living room — a medium-sized suitcase can only carry so much — and Una might well reappear. The double bed with posturepedic mattress was hers, two shelves of glossy books, mostly celebrity biographies, and a whole lot of junk in the sideboard. Perhaps she hadn't gone too far away, just far enough to feel hidden. What I needed most of all was someone to talk to about this sudden desertion, but the only person I really wanted to tell was Una herself.

When I located Roy's telephone number he sounded unsurprised to hear from me.

'Has Una been in touch with you?'

'I upset her, did I? Well, I warned you she'd let you down one day — run out on you, or worse.'

'Where's she gone?' I asked tersely, unprepared to listen to his monotonous voice go on and on.

'What?'

'You said she'd run out on me . . .'

'Well, sounds like that's what she's doing, isn't she? She wanted the name of my lawyer to set up some new arrangement about the flat — sorry, *apartment* — wasn't that it? She said it had been your idea to phone me.'

'So did you give her his name? Her name?'

A negative puffing noise sounded down the line. 'I've got a good relationship with Terence — I don't need Una mucking that up. What's wrong with the *Yellow Pages* if she doesn't like her own man, whoever he is? She got a bit ropey. I only got off lightly because she didn't want to wake you. It was the middle of the night, for goodness' sake! Tell her not to phone me again.'

I sat in a café over the road from the hospital and told Beryl some of this. She had bought a bunch of freesias that lay on the table between us, exuding a pungent smell that reminded me of David's funeral. Beryl was looking more like a wedding than a funeral guest, dressed in the smartest outfit I'd ever seen her wearing. I interrupted her flow of words to remark on this.

She blushed. 'I bought it for the school reunion and I haven't worn it since. But I felt like celebrating Sheree's new little life. Why not? Babies are born every minute, but this is ours, isn't it? Feels like ours anyway.' Her hand moved to finger the plastic carrier bag soft with a cuddly brown toy.

'I guess . . . I'm more concerned with breaking the news about Una emptying her stuff out of the wardrobe.'

'But that's good, isn't it? So that she can have the bigger room you said.'

'She's gone!' I exploded.

'I know, but — gone where?'

'I don't know where she's gone. That's the point. You haven't been listening to me!'

'I'm sorry. I just want to get to the hospital. I'm a bit taken up with this idea of being a godmother; it's really cheered me up. Oh, I know I'm not officially. But we can't call her our granddaughter can we? God-daughter sounds better.'

I plonked my cup down and propped my face in my hands to stop it sinking to the table. The freesias assailed my nostrils.

'I'm sorry,' Beryl repeated. 'Tell me again. I'm listening.'

'Where would she go? I mean, you can't hide, can you, not in Wellington or not for long. Her daughter's in America but she wouldn't go there.'

'Why not?'

'Apart from anything else she'd need a visa.'

'That's the baby's grandmother, isn't it? The real one. I'd forgotten her — she won't come over, will she? Does Sheree want her to?'

'I doubt it. She's religious, Sheree won't want that.'

Beryl looked clearly relieved.

I fell silent. I was mulling over how Jane, the daughter, might react to Una's news, supposing she was ever given access to it. 'She can be quite bossy, my Jane, even long distance,' Una had said.

Walking up through the car park Beryl said, 'I can't help

thinking it's good that she's gone. You're out of it, you can stop worrying about police and stuff.'

'I wanted to help her.'

'She has to help herself.'

'She can't. She's hopeless.'

'That's up to her. She'll do whatever she's going to do anyway. It's not your job, Clarice. She's not your responsibility or you'd have reported her to the police days ago.'

'I know. I know you're right. I'm going to miss her!' I heard my voice crooning despair as we entered the lift and a fat old man stared at us, careful not to let his face flicker with interest while we went on talking as if the lift were empty.

'You didn't even like her.'

'I did. Quite a lot — in bits. Anyway I'm a creature of habit.'

'We all are,' Beryl nodded and the old man looked as if he might nod with her. The lift was stationary at the wrong floor while a wheelchair was being trundled towards it.

'That's why I took so long getting out of my marriage to Lester, which was pretty hopeless from the start. I was glad to be free but even then it took me ages to get over the divorce. It was like I went into mourning for at least a year. Mad, eh?' I met Beryl's eyes and remembered her grief, which seemed to have gone on for decades. 'I mean since it was me who up and left,' I added. But Beryl was waiting for the lift doors to part with only the anticipation of pleasure on her face.

'Look what Una brought me.' These were nearly Sheree's first words as we entered the ward. She was standing beside the bed, unpacking soft blue folded wool from a drawstring bag.

'When? Has she been in?'

'This morning. You can wear the baby round your middle like a kangaroo. Isn't it neat?'

'I thought you wanted to get rid of your bum in front,' I teased her. 'So how was she?'

'Brenda? I haven't tried her in it yet.'

Beryl was busy murmuring over the sleeping infant.

'How was Una?' I needed to know.

'You know how she is. She was okay. No, she was rapt, I suppose. Not as daft as Beryl — sorry, Beryl — but she didn't say anything rude. She didn't stay long — had to get somewhere in a hurry. Why?' She focused on my expression. 'Has something happened?'

I was overtaken with the hopeful conviction that when I returned home Una would be there again, comfortably installed as she'd suggested in the little back bedroom, as small as a prison cell. Anything could happen — we were still waiting for the fat lady to sing. 'Not much. Nothing for you to worry about.'

'What does that mean?' She was looking at me too closely.

'I brought Brenda a cocker spaniel. It's plush — very soft,' Beryl said quickly.

Sunday evening. I was sitting alone in the burgundy armchair, listening to the wind in the kitchen extractor fan. Words came flurrying out of the sound of the wind, settling on me like tickertape before flying off again, leaving a new thought that did nothing to fill the emptiness. Soft, I remembered. The squashy brown dog the size of a newborn baby, the look on Beryl's face at the hospital. Victim, I remembered, one of Una's words describing her mother. 'Victims get raped, they get their throats cut.' A reference to her jailbird husband? 'That's not me,' she had said. But that wasn't exactly true. Una was a victim, just as Garth had been a victim, just as Beryl was soft, just as I could be hard, according to Una. I felt anything but hard now. It seemed people were condemned to try on many words in the dictionary, just not all at once. One after the other. I recalled Beryl's comment about names and words queuing up to be remembered. I didn't know which word was waiting to settle on me next and burrow into my brain so that I would have to take it to bed with me. Alone.

Such a scary word, alone. It belonged to everyone at some time in their life, unless they had tricked themselves with TV or booze or God. Alone we are born and die alone — someone clever said that a long time ago. Greta Garbo wanted to be alone, but she probably lied. People lie.

That was when a knock came at the door. I stood up slowly. I wasn't going to hurry and open up to the police, supposing this was the scene Una had been running from. A memory flash of Kevin's first time at the door, which had woken me from a dream of a television programme. It seemed a long time ago, that bathroom flood — I was younger then, although only months had passed. But it could be Kevin at the door again, I told myself. Think positively.

It was another lonely woman standing in the passage. Old Marge from upstairs — 'I'm made of the best butter actually'. Aloneness started out of her eyes and glinted from her white false teeth. She was holding a big white envelope like a ticket of admission. White for danger? I stood back and allowed her to come inside.

'What is it?'

'I was told to hold onto this until tonight, then to make sure you got it. Una. She gave it to me yesterday morning. I think it's something for the baby, is it?'

I took it. It was addressed to Clarice and Sheree. I

knew I should offer this woman a cup of tea; the old Clarice would have, but apparently not this one. I shook my head, putting the envelope on the bench. 'I'm sorry — I've got a bit of a head. Do you mind?'

It was a card, an outsize postcard with an unlikely koala bear clutching a wine bottle. On the back a brief message shouted in cheerful black letters: 'Guess where I'll be next week? I'll be having a lovely time and wishing you were here, like they say.' There were two keys in the envelope, one of them a car key. Una's Mazda. In much smaller letters in the bottom left-hand corner of the card one word spoke out: 'Sorry'.

I sat in the burgundy chair feeling the familiar clutch of the damaged spring against my left buttock. So. Australia. As good a place as any, I supposed, to wait for the authorities to come and find Una. And then? The chair held on to me. After tomorrow Sheree would claim this spot, the best chair she'd say to feed her baby in, but this wasn't what kept me attached to the corded velvet as if I'd been stitched there. There seemed so little reason to move. Was the show really over? What did I mean — over? Perhaps it was beginning again, like continuous pictures when I was a child.

In my head I consulted my diary. In the morning I would have to get up and go to work early. Monday would be a busy day because of last week's advertising mail drop about a free consultation. And after work I would look for the Mazda, probably parked around the corner in Ellice Street, and collect Sheree and the baby — with Beryl. It was good that Beryl would be there to help cushion the news of Una's farewell postcard just in case Sheree cared. Sheree had been Una's lame duck, not mine, although she claimed I was the duck collector and certainly I seemed to have collected Sheree. Una had said Beryl was a lame duck but perhaps she was confusing lame with elderly. The word fitted Beryl although she was only sixty-four. But Beryl was okay. Not everyone was untrustworthy. Not everyone told lies.

*Beryl was talking to Greg Preston in the bedroom mirror. 'Well, you said I'd lie when I had to and I'd make a fair job of it. Everyone does it, you said.'*